Awakening of the Beast

WES PHELAN

ISBN: 978-1-944878-72-6
Tiger Publishing LLC

CHAPTER ONE

The year was 1884, and the power of the British Empire was at its peak. It had been almost three months since we left the Himalayas. Our ship, the HMS *Narwhal*, was rounding the southern end of the Arabian Peninsula. We would soon enter the Red Sea and begin the last leg of our journey. Our final destination was the pyramids of Egypt.

After breakfast, Zhong, Mick and I joined the other passengers on the deck chairs. They were set under tarpaulins rigged by the crew to shade us from the burning sun. We took a cool drink from a passing steward and stared out at the dead-calm sea.

Mick stretched his long legs. He was an Australian and a head taller than everyone. "I got to be honest, John. The closer we get to England, the more you turn back into a snob."

"At the price of these fares," I said, "is it too much to ask that the eggs are done right?"

"After what we've eaten, I'd say the eggs were perfect." Mick pulled a pack of cards from his pocket. "Who's up for a game of poker?"

Zhong kept his eyes on the water. "I'm sorry, Mick. Monks do not gamble."

"And that's a shame," Mick said. "Beating you would be the ultimate challenge."

"I'll play," I said. "But only if you promise not to cheat."

"Fine." Mick began shuffling the cards. "I promise, at least for the first game."

The three of us were an unlikely group of mates. Zhong was a Tibetan monk. Mick was the son of an Irish criminal. And I was the son of a wealthy British aristocrat. Despite our differences, we had a friendship forged in the furnace of shared dangers and stronger than the bond of brothers.

"Off the port bow!" a crewman yelled, pointing west.

Any break in the monotony was welcome. Everyone walked to the railing, and we joined them. A thin line stretched along the western horizon. Discussions began immediately as to what it was. Most of the passengers thought it was Africa.

I shielded my eyes against the sun. "What do you think, Zhong?"

"Africa is too far to see."

"Then what is it?"

"Something I have never seen before."

"Well, whatever that is," Mick said, "It's growing."

Suddenly, Zhong ran across the deck.

"Where're you going?" I asked.

Zhong stopped below the wheelhouse and waved up at a bearded face behind the glass. "Captain!"

The captain leaned out the open hatch. "What is it, Mr. Zhong?"

Zhong pointed to the west. "Captain! What you see is a tsunami! Steer directly toward it. It is our only chance!"

The captain squinted at the horizon, and his eyes went wide. He pulled his head back inside and slammed the hatch shut.

AHOOO-GA! AHOOO-GA! AHOOO-GA! The ship's alarm sounded as the bow veered abruptly to port and aimed for the tsunami.

Zhong picked up a coil of line and turned to the passengers. "A giant wave is about to hit the ship! We must tie ourselves to the railing behind the staterooms. Follow me!"

We ran to the stern, followed by four crewmen and forty-five passengers. Everyone else stayed on the foredeck and watched the wave. I wanted to go back and convince the others to follow Zhong, but there was no more time for words.

We halted in the stern. Zhong quickly cut the line into lengths with his knife and then passed them out. "Use this to tie your chest to the railing," he said. "Then wrap your arms through the railing. Just before the wave hits, take a deep breath—and hold it!"

Every face was filled with confusion and fear. Zhong, Mick, the crewmen and I helped the passengers struggling to make a knot. Out of the corner of my eye I saw Zhong's hands move so fast they were a blur.

Then I heard an outburst of shouts and screams from the bow.

"Let me in!"

"We'll die out here!"

"Lord, save us!"

I stepped to where I could see around the staterooms. Passengers were shoving and fighting to get inside the ship. Crewmen were jumping into the forward hold. Beyond the ship was a wall of green, foaming water as tall as a three-story building.

I turned back to Zhong. "We need to be inside with the others!"

"No. The ship will fill with water. Tie yourself to the railing now!"

"Just do it, John!" Mick said. "When has Zhong ever been wrong?"

I pushed into the space beside Zhong. I had just started my second knot when I heard a deafening roar, and the deck tilted upward to almost vertical. A wall of green water crowned with froth towered above the ship. The wave tipped over and plummeted down onto the deck. I yanked on the knot to tighten it, grabbed the railing and took a deep breath.

Water smashed me and squeezed the air from my lungs. I gritted my teeth to keep from breathing in water. The ship raced upward and slammed me against the deck. I felt the line slip across my chest. My hands were ripped from the railing. I was about to be swept away when my wrist caught on something, and I flailed in the streaming water. My lungs burned. Just when I was about to inhale water, the ship broke through the wave like a massive cork.

I was tossed into the air. I took a quick breath before crashing onto the deck. The ship rocked violently to one side, and I grabbed the railing with my free hand. I held on as the ship swung hard in the other direction then held my breath, expecting more water.

The ship continued swinging back and forth, and I let myself breathe. The rocking gradually slowed until all that remained was the normal swaying of the sea. That is when I looked to see what had caught my wrist. Zhong was motionless beside me, his right hand wrapped around my wrist. He was still tied to the railing. Unlike me, his knots had held.

Zhong opened his eyes and released his grip. "I almost lost you, John."

"But you didn't. Thank you, Zhong—again." He had saved Mick and me so many times our debt to him could never be repaid.

I ignored the pain of my battered body and forced myself up onto one elbow. "Mick!" I tried to shout, but his name came out as a low rasp.

A hand rose on the other side of the deck and gave a limp wave. Mick was alive, and we had survived. I looked over the ship.

The deck had been swept clean except for the bodies still tied to the bent railings. Most of the bodies were motionless, but some moved and groaned. All the lifeboats were gone. The deck tilted down to the bow and to starboard, and the bow and starboard deck were both below water. The hatch of the aft hold was gone. Water filled the hold to within two feet of the opening. The roof over the staterooms had been ripped away. Hissing steam poured up from where the smokestack had been.

The water around the ship was calm but filled with floating debris and bodies. I looked for the tsunami. It was now a thin line on the eastern horizon that disappeared as I watched.

Zhong pulled his last knot apart. "John, help Mick. Then help the other survivors."

He walked down the deck to a woman who was groaning. I stumbled up the deck toward Mick. He was undoing his last knot.

"So much for our relaxing sea voyage," he said.

"Zhong wants us to help the other survivors."

Mick stood with a grunt. "We're lucky there's anyone left to help."

We spent the next hours untying knots and bandaging wounds with strips of torn clothing. After helping survivors on the aft deck, Zhong, Mick and I walked toward the bow looking for more. Like the aft deck, the forward deck had been stripped clean, and the hatch for the forward hold was missing. The water inside the forward hull was inches from the top and thick with floating bodies.

Zhong pointed to small waves that pushed up the deck where it dipped into the sea. The tip of each wave added more water to the hold. "The waves will sink the ship. When we finish looking for survivors, we must begin bailing."

I opened a hatch into the staterooms. Water rushed out, bringing seven bodies with it. The inside passageway was packed with more dead.

"Good lord," I whispered.

To search the inside of the ship for survivors, we had to step on and over the bodies. We looked into every compartment and the saloon. Just as Zhong predicted, no one inside the ship survived. Our last stop was the wheelhouse. Mick led the way up the ladder. Water poured out when he opened the hatch. The glass in the windows was gone, except for sharp fragments around the edges. The motionless bodies of the captain and the two crewmen had been thrown against the rear bulkhead.

We returned to the stern to organize the survivors for bailing. I counted seventeen passengers and four crewmen sitting or lying on the deck. Including the three of us, that made a total of twenty-four survivors. Before the tsunami, there had been 164 passengers and a crew of 28 souls.

Zhong pointed to Mr. Harley, the third mate and the only remaining ship's officer. He had been unconscious when we left. He was now sitting with his back to the railing and his head between his knees. "We must ask Mr. Harley to organize us for bailing out the water. Since I am the servant, one of you should ask."

"I'll do it," Mick said.

We sat beside Harley. He looked at us, his face filled with fear.

"Mr. Harley," Mick said. "We just checked the ship, and we have a problem in the bow. We're taking on water. If we don't start bailing, we're going to sink. The only survivors are the ones you see here."

"Why tell me?" Harley asked.

"You're the last officer," I said. "The order has to come from you."

Harley dropped his head. "I can't."

"What do mean you can't?" I asked.

"Well, if you can't, I can, Mr. Harley," Mick said. "With your permission, of course."

Harley nodded, his head facing down.

Mick stood. "All right, everybody, listen up." He waited until he had everyone's attention. "This ship's already filled with water and taking on more. If we don't start bailing, we're going to sink. And if we sink, we're going to die! I want everyone to find something that holds water, the bigger the better. Then start bailing out the forward hold."

A man sitting next to Mick shook his head. "No."

Mick turned to face him. "What do you mean 'no'?"

"We almost died," the man said. "We need a little time to recover."

"Get on your feet," Mick ordered.

"I told you, no."

"We don't have time for this," Mick said. He kicked the man in his buttocks and knocked him over. The startled man quickly got to his feet. The rest of the survivors, including Harley, also stood.

"Follow me," Mick said, leading the survivors to the foredeck.

"You like kicking people, don't you?" I whispered.

"Only when they need it," Mick replied.

The only things left that could hold water were inside the ship. Once again, we had to step on bodies to find them. Soon we were lowering small barrels, metal bowls, mugs, pitchers and even a small wooden chest into the forward hold. We pushed them between the floating bodies, scooped out the water and tossed it into the sea. As we worked, the sun we had enjoyed just hours before made us hot and miserable and sapped our strength.

After an hour of steady bailing, Mick pointed into the hold. "That water level is higher than when started."

"The water we remove is replaced by the waves," Zhong said. "We must block them."

"With what?" I asked. "Everything's gone."

"We will use our dead."

The survivors heard Zhong and stopped bailing. His suggestion felt wrong and sacrilegious, but no one said a word. Everyone knew there was no other option.

Zhong reached into the hold and grabbed the ankle of a floating sailor. I forced myself to hold the man's wrist. With everyone watching, we pulled the body from the hold and dragged it to where the waves came up the deck. The next wave swept over and around the body into the hold. Zhong and I pulled out a second body and placed it head to foot in line with the first one. The next wave was partially blocked, with most of the water still sweeping around the bodies.

Mick nudged Harley and grabbed the wrist of a dead crewman. Harley reluctantly took the ankle. The other survivors began reaching into the hold and the passageway, pulling out more bodies and adding them to the pile.

After twenty minutes of dragging bodies into a pile, a wave swept up the deck, hit the bodies and slipped back into the sea.

"That's it! We've done it!" Mick cried. "Back to bailing!"

After more hours of working in the hot sun, survivors were staggering, and the water inside the hold was only inches lower. A woman collapsed, followed quickly by a man. Soon everyone was sitting or lying on the deck. We needed water, but there wasn't any. The freshwater barrels in the galley had been smashed against the bulkheads.

Zhong, Mick and I sat beside Harley.

"Mr. Harley," Zhong said, "the water barrels are stored in the forward hold, are they not?"

Harley nodded. "I think it's straight down from the hatch, but I'm not sure."

"That's ridiculous!" I said. "You're a ship's officer, and you don't know where the water is?"

"You can't get to them anyway! They're under twenty-five feet of water!"

"Is there a ship's pump?" Zhong asked.

Harley dropped his eyes.

"Do you know the location?" Zhong pressed.

Harley nodded and pointed forward. "It's in the bow, sitting on the main beam. I have to warn you. There's no air, and it's black as pitch down there."

"We must try to get it," Zhong said. He stepped through the hatch to the cabins.

"So, there's a pump, is there?" Mick said to Harley "We're killing ourselves, and you don't even mention it?"

"There wasn't any point! You can't reach it!"

Zhong returned with a coil of line. He tied one end around his abdomen and handed the other end to Mick. "Mr. Harley, please describe the pump."

"On top of it are two coils of canvas hose. The hoses and a long wooden handle are tied to a thick metal pipe. The pipe is the pump."

Zhong sat on the edge of the hatch. He pushed away the floating bodies with his feet and slid feet first into the water. He took a large breath and dove, disappearing into the blackness of the hold. Mick fed out the line to keep it loose.

It was two long minutes before Zhong's head broke the water's surface, gasping. "I found it."

"How did you do that?" Harley asked.

"It is enough that I did. You can pull it up."

Mick, Harley and I took hold of the line and stepped backwards until a crewman looking into the open hatch shouted, "Stop!"

The crewmen took hold of the line, and we walked to the hold. Below the water's surface were two coils of hose. We lifted them out, along with the attached wooden handle and pump. Mick pulled out his knife and cut the lines holding everything together, and we unrolled the hoses. We looked at Harley for the next step.

"I don't exactly remember what goes where," Harley said.

"Do you know anything about this ship?" I asked.

"I only had a brief instruction when I entered the merchant marine," Harley admitted.

"We will help you, Mr. Harley," Zhong said.

"Again," Mick muttered.

Zhong and Harley attached the wooden handle to a metal pivot on top of the pipe. Mick and I screwed the ends of the hoses onto the pipe. At Zhong's direction, I placed the end of my hose into the flooded hold. Mick positioned his hose where it would drain into the sea.

With the crewmen holding the pump below the water in the hold, Zhong and Harley pumped the handle up and down like a seesaw. At first, it did nothing but make a loud squeaking noise. When it made a sputtering sound, all eyes focused on the end of the drain hose. A small amount of water spurted from the hose and slid down the deck to the sea. Everyone cheered.

With the pump primed and ready, it was placed on the deck. We rotated manning the pump in teams of two. The rest of us continued scooping water out of the hold. When the water level was too low to reach from the hatch, someone stood on the ladder inside the hold. He scooped up the water and passed it to a waiting hand.

By early afternoon, the water in the hold was seven feet below the hatch opening. The bow and the starboard edges of the deck were at the water's surface. Everyone was now lightheaded and staggering,

"Tell the people to stop," Zhong said. "It is time to find a water barrel."

"Okay, everyone, take a rest!" Mick called out.

Zhong, Mick, Harley and I sat down together.

Mick looked at Harley. "You said the water barrels are straight down from the hatch."

"What I said was, I think that's where they are."

"Let's assume we find an intact barrel," Mick said. "How do we lift it out? They're heavy."

"A barrel filled with water is weight neutral in water," Harley said. "We tie a line around it and haul it to the surface."

"That still leaves seven feet to go," I pointed out.

"Then we lift it out the way it went in: with a block and tackle."

"Don't tell me," Mick said. "It's in the hold with everything else, and you don't know where it is."

"No," Harley said, "the block and tackle are in a locker behind the saloon. And that, Mr. Kelly, is something I know how to use."

"And about bloody time, too," Mick said.

Harley and the crewmen went to get the block and tackle. With the other survivors watching, Zhong, Mick and I climbed down the ladder into the hold. It still looked dark below us, but we needed water, and we had to try. Zhong pushed the dead bodies to the side as Mick and I slipped into the water.

Something touched my leg. I grunted and twisted away.

"Hold my shirt," Zhong said. "Follow me down. When we reach the bottom, look for a barrel with the word 'water'."

Mick and I grabbed Zhong's shirt. We took a deep breath and dove straight down. I did my best to ignore the bumps and touches of the dead sailors. But when a lifeless hand brushed my face, I panicked and let go of Zhong. My arms flailed until I found his shirt.

It was murky at the bottom. We picked through broken wood in search of an intact barrel. My lungs were burning when I picked up a long piece. I could barely make out the white-stenciled letters "TER." I tapped Zhong and held it up. He nodded and pointed to the surface. It was time for air.

We broke the surface with loud gasps.

"We found the water barrels!" I rasped to the people watching.

There was a hoarse cheer.

Over the hatch pulleys and lines hung from a wooden A-frame. Harley and a crewman were feeding the lines through the pulleys.

Harley tossed lines with loops at the end to Zhong and Mick. They slipped the loops around their chests.

"Gentlemen, we're ready when you are," Harley said.

"Nice work, Mr. Harley," Mick said.

We took deep breaths and dove again. The crewmen fed out the lines as we descended. We reached the bottom and quickly cleared out pieces of wood, until we found an intact barrel with "WATER" barely visible on the side. We pulled it over on its side. Zhong and Mick slipped the loops over the ends of the barrel and tugged them tight. Our lungs burning, we raced for the surface and burst from the water.

"Now Mr. Harley," Zhong said.

"Ladies! Gentlemen!" Harley called out. "You may now pull."

Both lines were held by six-person teams of men and women. The teams began stepping backwards. Zhong, Mick and I remained in the water to guide the barrel from below. When the barrel reached the water's surface, there was another cheer.

The teams kept backing up until the barrel was inches above the hatch. That's when Zhong, Mick

15

and I climbed out of the hold. Crewmen pulled the barrel onto the deck and rolled it up on one end. Harley quickly popped off the top with a pry bar. Using anything that would hold water, including our cupped hands, everyone dipped into the water and drank. The barrel was half empty before we had quenched our thirst. Then we laid on the deck and savored the moment.

Mick sighed. "If we just had something to eat, everything would be perfect."

Harley stood. "Mr. Kelley, Mr. Sexton, Mr. Zhong, please, follow me."

We followed Harley to the stern. The aft deck was covered with kernel corn drying in the sun. A pile of empty, wet burlap bags was off to one side.

"When did you do this?" I asked.

"While you dove for the barrel, I had the passengers search for food," Harley said. "Most of it's ruined, but there was corn, small barrels of pickles, tins of biscuits and chocolate."

"Chocolate?" Mick smiled and grabbed Harley's shoulder. "Well done, sir."

When we finished our feast, the light was gone, except for a dark red streak to the west. The sky was black and filled with stars. We lay on the deck, enjoying our full stomachs and a hard-earned sleep.

I was drifting off when Mick whispered from beside me, "I haven't heard you complain about the meal yet. I assumed the corn would be too hard for your liking."

"All right, you've made your point," I said. "I've been a little too picky."

"A little?"

"Maybe more than a little. I'll try to do better." Now that I was awake, I became aware of a foul stench. "I know I just said I wouldn't complain, but do you smell some bad meat?"

Mick nodded. "Yeah. It's getting stronger."

"That is our dead," Zhong said. His shadow was sitting on the other side of Mick, staring at the sea. "Bodies rot quickly in the hot sun. We must deal with our dead, but that can wait until the light."

"Zhong, is the smell why aren't you sleeping?" I asked

"I sense something I cannot name."

"I hope it's not another tsunami," Mick said

"No. This is evil. Do not wait on me. Sleep while you can."

We began the tasks at dawn, with anyone not working the pump tossing bodies overboard. Mick and I had just thrown our ninth body into the sea when we heard a loud splash. We looked toward the sound but saw nothing except debris and floating bodies.

Mick pointed. "There!"

A triangular gray fin glided between the bodies and dropped out of sight. Seconds later, there was churning and splashing. A human head popped up and swung around in a wide circle before plunging below the surface. Our eyes tracked where the head had disappeared, not wanting to watch but unable to look away.

A woman and a man threw a body into the water and stopped to watch with us. Minutes later, the body bobbed to the surface and rolled, revealing a stump where an arm had been. The woman shrieked.

"Look at all of them!" the man shouted.

Eight triangular fins slid in among the bodies. Our burial at sea had become a feast for sharks. We had no choice but to ignore the sick feeling in our gut and add another body to the carnage.

As we continued throwing the bodies overboard, the number of sharks grew. The splashing and thrashing became more intense. Mick and I carried the bodies with our eyes down to avoid seeing the carnage, but there was no way to block the sound.

By noon, all the dead were floating in the sea. Zhong had us sit with Harley and the crewmen to discuss our next move. We tried to ignore the thrashing of the sharks.

"Mr. Harley, by its size and direction, the tsunami has destroyed every ship in its path," Zhong said. "There will not be a ship to save us. We must save ourselves, starting now."

"You're talking about starting the steam engine," Harley said. "It's still underwater, and there's bound to be damage."

"Actually, most of the engine is out of the water," Mick said. "I just checked it."

"By tomorrow, it'll all be above water," a crewman added.

"I suggest we inspect the engine now," Zhong said. "If we repair the damage we find, we'll be that much closer to starting it. Once the water is below the engine, we inspect the rest, and there will be that much less to fix."

Harley nodded. "You're right again, Mr. Zhong."

"Assuming we can start the engine, where do we go?" I asked.

"An excellent question, John," Mick replied.

Zhong looked at Harley. "Do you have any suggestions, Mr. Harley?"

"I do," Harley said. "But first I need to point out that a patch on the boiler is just that, a patch. The only real fix is a weld, and we can't do them. That means we need to make landfall before the boiler blows. And we need to be somewhere we can get help."

Mick nodded. "Makes sense. So, where is this place?"

"I have to check the charts, but Djibouti may be our only choice."

"And where's that?" I asked.

"Africa. Due west."

"Isn't that the direction the tsunami came from?" Mick asked.

"It is," Zhong said. "Time to inspect the engine."

The three of us and the crewmen followed Harley down the ladder into the aft hold. The engine and boiler were sitting in three feet of water. We waded around them as the crewmen pointed out problems, like bent and separated pipes. The only serious damage was the partial separation of a metal seam on the boiler.

"Sir, with your permission," a crewman said to Harley, "we'll start patching the boiler and fixing those pipes."

"You may begin, men," Harley said. "Anything else we should do, gentlemen?"

"We'll need fuel for the boiler," Zhong said.

"Thank you, Mr. Zhong," Harley said. "I'll have the passengers spread the coal out on the deck to dry."

For the rest of the day and through the night, teams of two continued pumping the water out of the hold. At the first light of dawn, everyone was staring into the dark hold. We were anxious to see if we had pumped out enough water for a final verdict on damages to the engine and boiler. When there was enough light to see, the water was several inches below both. The crew climbed down and circled the engine and boiler, occasionally stopping to touch or pull something.

After their second trip around, Mick called down. "So, what's the word?"

A crewman looked up. "No sign of any more damage. Sir, permission to fill the boiler and the fire box!"

"Permission granted," Harley said. "You may fire the boiler when you're ready."

Everyone watched as crewman filled the boiler with water and placed coal and kindling wood inside the firebox. A crewman reached inside the firebox, and I heard a scraping sound as he struck a flint. He pulled his hands out and blew softly. A thin trail of gray smoke drifted up from the open grate, followed by crackling. He closed the grate, smiled and gave us a thumbs-up. We all cheered.

Sparks floated up from the hole where the smokestack had been. Without the stack to funnel them away, the sparks floated onto the wooden deck. We couldn't let a fire start, because there would be no escape, especially with sharks in the water. Harley had everyone carry a container filled with seawater. The survivors closest to the sparks doused them quickly.

There was a rumbling inside the boiler, followed by pops and a low-pitched moan. I turned to Harley. "Is the patch coming apart?"

"No. Those are the sounds a boiler always makes when it starts up. When a patch fails, it makes a loud hiss, like a tea kettle."

After what felt like hours, a crewman in the hold shouted, "Boiler ready, sir!"

"Permission to start the engine!" Harley said and climbed the ladder to the wheelhouse.

The crewman reached up and rotated a large shut-off valve on the pipe from the boiler to the engine. The valve squealed with each turn. Clanking sounds came from the engine. Minutes later, we heard a slow thumping that sped up. It was followed by thrashing water behind the stern.

The ship eased forward. We applauded and cheered as our ship limped toward Africa, still tilting to starboard.

CHAPTER TWO

In the middle of the night, I was jerked out of my sleep. The world was pitch black, except for the stars filling the sky. I heard a loud groan, followed by a high-pitched hiss. I knew immediately the patch on the boiler seam was failing. Then came a banging noise.

"Zhong, what is that?"

"The crew's hammering plugs into the split," Harley said from the darkness.

The hiss became softer, but it did not stop. I felt the ship slow.

"There's nothing else we can do," Harley said.

I lay back down but couldn't sleep. I kept waiting for the hiss to grow louder.

Everyone was in the bow when the first morning light appeared. We had gotten through the night without a change in hissing, but we weren't out of trouble. Thick gray clouds filled the sky to the west.

Harley joined us in the bow. "I checked the boiler. No change from last night, but it won't survive a storm."

"Can we sail around it?" Mick asked.

"That'll take two days at least. The boiler won't last another day, even without a storm. And Africa is our closest land."

"So, what do we do?" I asked.

"When there is only one choice," Zhong said, "you choose it."

We continued sailing west toward land and the storm.

As we approached the tempest, we kept expecting strong winds and rough seas, but the air and the water remained oddly calm. It was late afternoon when we sailed under the gray cloud, and the world turned to dusk. The air had a faint smell of smoke and sulfur. Instead of rain, what came down was a fine gray ash that covered everything.

"This isn't a storm," I said, wiping the ash from my shoulder and examining my fingers.

"There is an active volcano ahead," Zhong said. "Eruptions cause earthquakes. Tsunamis are made by earthquakes."

Mick chuckled. "The good news is, there's nothing left to go wrong."

A loud bang was followed by steam billowing up from the aft hold.

"It's coming apart!" a crewman cried.

Mick rolled his eyes. "Me and my big mouth."

Everyone ran to the stern. Steam was pouring out of the hold. The split in the boiler seam was hard to see with boiling water and steam spewing from the opening. The crew used mallets to jab wooden plugs into the seam. It reduced the leak but didn't stop it. The ship slowed to a crawl. It was another long tense day as we waited for the boiler to fail.

It was early dusk when a crewman shouted, "There's land ahead!"

Ahead of us on the horizon were scattered pin-points of red light. It had to be the town of Djibouti. To the right of the town was a wide body of water. High above Djibouti was the glowing red peak of an active volcano. A column of smoke boiled up from the volcano into the cloud overhead.

"What do you think, Zhong?" Mick asked. "Will we make it?"

"It will be close," Zhong said.

"And if we don't make it?" I asked.

"Then we swim," Mick said.

I looked up to the wheelhouse. Harley was inside with both hands on the wheel. He was steering straight for the lights and a jetty of piled rocks.

A sudden loud clanging came from the boiler. The crew leapt from the hold just ahead of a billowing cloud of white steam. All engine sounds stopped, except for a loud, steady hiss.

Everyone held their breath as the ship drifted closer to the jetty. When the ship bumped it, Zhong, Mick and I jumped onto the jetty. The crew threw us the ship's lines, and we quickly secured them to the rocks.

Djibouti was a cluster of small single-story huts made from mud and bricks. Many of them were partially collapsed. Others were on fire, with rising columns of smoke. Gray volcanic ash covered everything, including the Africans. The people looked like thin gray ghosts as they sat or walked. The men were bare-chested with pants that ended in tatters at the knee. The women wore robes with frayed edges.

I turned back to the ship. Harley and the other survivors were still on board, their eyes fixed on the town. That's when I realized that everyone, including the three of us, looked like gray ghosts, too.

"What're you waiting for?" Mick shouted at the survivors. "Get off the ship. We made it!"

No one moved.

Mick turned to Zhong and me. "I don't know about you, but I'm ready to eat something besides pickles and hard corn."

I nodded. "We're right behind you."

Mick led us across the jetty to a small shop facing the water. Inside was a short table with a flat loaf of bread and two black bananas. Standing beside the table was a man with a machete. He raised the large blade and eyed us suspiciously.

I showed the man the two British coins I had left. "You're waiting for this, I assume."

The man snatched them from my hand and gestured for us to sit on the bench. Soon we were feasting on dry bread and black bananas and clay cups filled with something sour. I looked back at the ship. The other survivors were hard to see in the fading light, but they were still on board.

I choked down the last of my drink just as an old African man walked in front of the shop. He carried a torch and a cloth bag. He dropped the bag and drove the torch into the ground, studying our faces with open curiosity. The old man was as tall as Mick but much thinner. Unlike everyone else, there was no ash on him or his robe. Even odder was the sharp contrast between the man's pale blue eyes, black skin and the long white hair of his head and beard.

"This man is unique," Zhong said.

Mick nodded. "He's different all right."

"It is not just the physical."

A group of Africans formed around the man. The shop owner raised his machete and watched the crowd, glancing occasionally at the old man.

The man reached into his bag and pulled out a long, hissing cobra. He held the snake out to us and then the crowd before dropping it inside the sack. He spoke words I did not recognize and pulled the snake out of the bag. Now it had two heads, one on each end, both biting the air and hissing angrily.

The crowd cheered and clapped. Mick and I clapped with them. The man was a magician and unusually skilled.

"Now that's what I call a trick," Mick said.

"That is not a trick," Zhong replied. "The snake has been physically changed."

I studied the creature. "That's impossible."

The magician dropped the snake back into the sack and spoke different words. This time when he removed the snake, it had a tail on both ends and no head. The tails wiggled furiously, and the crowd laughed.

The magician dropped the snake into the sack a third time. He pulled it out without a word, and the snake was back to normal, with a head on one end and a tail on the other. The snake sagged in the magician's hand as if exhausted by the transformations. Mick and I applauded along with the crowd.

"This man is young," Zhong said.

I didn't understand what he meant. But then I realized the magician's skin was smooth. I had assumed he was old because of his white hair and beard.

The magician lowered the snake into the bag and looked at us. "This is for you," he said with a strong African accent.

He reached into a pocket and removed a handful of red powder. He poured the powder onto the ground, forming a small pile shaped like a cone. The magician waved both hands over the powder. A blue flame flared at the tip and then was replaced by a thin trace of smoke. The smoke rose straight up until it was several feet above the magician's head.

The magician passed his right hand through the smoke. It thickened at the middle and formed a man's head with empty holes where the eyes should have been. The mouth hung open as if the head was screaming. The magician swept his left hand through the smoke. The smoke head and the column swirled like a top and then began to slow. When it stopped, the smoke had become a dragon, its head near the ground and the tail twisted upward. The crowd muttered, obviously afraid.

Angry shouts came from somewhere to our left. The crowd glanced toward the voices and ran to the right. The shop owner gave us a quick stare before running after them.

The magician put his hands together and bowed his head. The dragon dissolved and became a thin column of smoke. The magician picked up his bag and looked at us. "You must leave now."

The top of the smoke column bent over and engulfed him from his head to his toes. The smoke returned upright, and the magician was gone. The smoke dissipated, leaving a small patch of white ash.

We stood there, intending to follow the crowd, but before we could take a step, a large mob of men ran up and surrounded the front of the shop. The men were covered with ash, like everyone else. Some of them had torches, but they all had machetes and the same tattoo. It was exactly like the dragon in the smoke trick. The dragon's head and neck were on the left side of their chests. Its body extended over their left shoulders. The tail twisted up the left side of their necks and faces and ended on their foreheads. The mob began chanting the same words over and over.

"Follow me!" Zhong whispered.

We banged through a back door into a narrow dirt road and ran from the mob. The angry shouts of men poured into the road behind us. Men raced around the huts to get at us. We stopped abruptly when men with torches filled the road ahead.

Zhong led us into a small space between two buildings on our left. The space dead-ended and left us visible from the road. I turned to leave, but Mick's hand on my shoulder stopped me.

The mobs came together outside our space, swinging machetes and turning in circles, trying to see where we had gone. Several men looked into our space but didn't see us and then left. One man stepped inside. He halted with his face just inches from mine and still didn't see me. I knew Zhong was using meditation to control their minds and make us invisible. He had done it many times. But that did not stop the panic growing inside me. It was a relief when the man left.

After several tense minutes, the mob gave a shout and ran off to the left. When the shouting became faint, Zhong whispered, "We must leave."

We stepped back into the road but froze when the head of a boy popped up inside a collapsed hut.

He looked around before whispering, "Master say come."

"Who is your master?" Zhong replied.

"Simon master." The boy gestured for us to follow and ran away from the mob.

The boy was quick. Zhong matched his pace, but Mick and I had trouble keeping up. He led us through a maze of dirt streets and the narrow spaces between huts. When the boy threw himself behind a pile of rubble, we jumped in behind him. We dropped our heads just before another mob of men with dragon tattoos ran past.

When they were gone, the boy led us into a nearby alley, where he opened a door and waved us inside, then silently closed the door behind us.

We were in total darkness.

"What do we do, Zhong?" I asked.

"The boy has earned our trust," Zhong said. "We will wait for his return."

We dropped to the dirt floor. Occasionally, we heard the shouts of the mobs, but it was always in the distance.

Time is hard to judge in darkness, but after what seemed like an hour, there was a soft knock. Mick and I bolted to our feet, thinking the mob had found us.

"Dragon men do not knock," a voice said beside us.

"Who are you?" Mick asked.

"A friend."

A small flame appeared and grew slowly. It revealed a candle on the floor and then the long white hair and beard of the magician. He was sitting with his back to the wall. We were in a square room without windows. In the center of the floor was a black fire pit. In the roof above the fire pit was a round hole

"Enter, Bhotu," the magician said.

The door eased open. The boy who had led us there staggered into the room carrying a large basket. He lowered it to the floor and, unable to hold it any longer, dropped it.

"Thank you, Bhotu."

The boy left quickly and closed the door behind him. The magician pointed to the basket. "This is for you."

Mick eyed it warily. "That isn't a snake, is it?"

The magician smiled. "No. Only water, bread and cheese. Please, eat. You are safe here."

Mick lifted the lid and gave the inside a good look before pulling out a round flatbread. He broke off a piece and offered it to the magician.

"Thank you, but no. I have begun my fast."

"I hope this doesn't sound ungrateful," I said, taking a piece and handing the bread to Zhong, "but I have to ask: is there any way to help the people on our ship?"

The magician shook his head slowly. "I am sorry. They are already dead. The dragon men kill all strangers. They kill anyone who stands against them. They also kill his family, burn his home."

"Who are the dragon men?" Zhong asked.

"They are an ancient cult. They worship the dragon god, the god who sleeps. They believe their god will awaken one day and rule the world. They have a prophecy that the eruption of Tadjoura begins the god's awakening. The followers have always been few. But since the eruption, they number in the thousands. More arrive each day."

The magician rested his head against the wall. "We should introduce ourselves. I am Simon."

I extended my hand. "John Sexton."

Simon kept his hands at his side. "Do not be offended, John Sexton. I am honored to meet you and your friends, but my fast includes avoiding human touch."

Mick waved. "Friends call me Mick."

"Then I shall call you Mick." Simon looked at Zhong. "And you, sir?"

"I am Zhong, their servant."

"No, Zhong," Simon said. "You may serve them. But you are not their servant."

"I wish to know how you changed the snake," Zhong said, "and created the figures in the smoke."

Simon smiled. "You saw how I did it. I'm a magician."

"A magician performs illusions," Zhong replied. "Those were not illusions."

"I call it magic, because I don't know what else to call it. How the magic happens, I do not know. I am merely the vessel through which it happens.

33

I do not control it. It appears when and where it chooses. It never repeats itself. "

I shook my head. "That doesn't make any sense."

Simon shrugged. "I cannot explain what I do not understand."

"Have you always had the magic?" Mick asked.

"No. It started the day I left the orphanage. Before that, I was just another orphan, except for my hair and my eyes. And my dreaming of the same two dreams each night."

"One of your dreams is the eruption of a volcano," Zhong said.

Simon paused. "You are correct. How did you know?"

"The movement of Destiny is clear. The volcano's eruption created the tsunami. The tsunami forced us to sail here, to Djbouti."

"I assume you have already guessed the other dream."

"The second dream is about our arrival."

Simon smiled. "Well done, Zhong. Three men arriving from the sea. One is taller than I am. One is Oriental. The third is difficult to see. Their arrival marks the beginning of my destiny. And so, ever since the eruption of Tadjouri, I have watched the water."

Simon pointed to three bags in a corner. "Those are supplies Bhotu prepared for your journey. You are safe while you remain in this hut. But in the morning, while it is still dark, you must leave. I must leave now."

With those words, Simon slid backwards into the wall and disappeared. I felt the wall and the floor where he had been sitting and found nothing. I looked at the others in bewilderment. "He's gone!"

Mick looked at Zhong. "Was he controlling our minds the way you can?"

Zhong shook his head. "No, he was physically here."

"Then how did he leave?" I asked.

"I expect his magic took him."

"So, what do we do now?" Mick asked

"We follow Simon's advice," Zhong replied. "We rest after we finish our meal, and leave before dawn."

I reached into the basket and pulled out a hunk of cheese. I gave it a sniff. "This has gone bad."

"So, you're back to being picky?" Mick said, reaching for it. "Then I'll eat your share, too."

I pulled it back. "Not so fast, Mick. Zhong, is this safe to eat?"

"Considering the source, I'm certain it is," Zhong replied.

I broke off a third of the cheese before handing it to Mick. I took a small bite and tried not to gag. "So, we leave in the morning and go where?" I asked after chewing and swallowing it.

"I say we find another ship," Mick said, "and continue our visit to the pyramids."

"According to the charts, the nearest coastal town is to the south," Zhong said. "Simon said this room is safe. But caution demands that one of us sleeps in front of the door."

Mick bit off a mouthful of cheese. He gagged, too, and tried to hide it. "Zhong, what did you think of the smoke tricks?"

Zhong put his fingertips together below his chin. "Very interesting."

"The dragon was exactly like the one in the Sanctuary," I said.

"So were the tattoos," Mick added.

"Despite the distance between them, they must come from the same source," Zhong said.

I looked at him. "Maybe your ancestors worshipped a dragon."

"I am not aware that they did," Zhong replied. "I do know they pursued evil before following Buddha."

I watched Zhong take a bite of cheese. He gave the remaining cheese a long look before taking another.

Hours later, we crept outside. Everything was pitch black, except for scattered fires. Zhong led us through the town, sometimes walking fast, sometimes running, but always heading south. The horizon to the east had turned red, signaling the approaching dawn.

We had just passed the edge of town and emerged onto a wide open plain when a hundred points of light flared in the blackness ahead.

"What is that?" I asked.

Zhong stopped. "Dragon men."

"Looks like they were waiting for us," Mick said.

The torches began bouncing as the men ran toward us.

"We must hide in the town," Zhong said. "After they pass, we will start again."

We ran back into the town, looking for a place to hide. We were less than a hundred yards inside when more dragon men carrying torches poured into the road ahead.

Suddenly, flashes of light blinded us. I barely made out clouds of sparkling smoke billowing up in front and behind us. The dragon men caught in the smoke screamed and covered their eyes with their hands.

The door of a hut opened. Simon stepped out and waved us in. He closed the door behind us. It was pitch black inside.

"Please sit," he whispered. "Do not speak."

We sat and listened to the dragon men's screams and angry shouts. When the sounds died away, we heard the scrape of a flint and saw red sparks. A flame flared at the top of a candle. We were in another small room, but unlike the first one, it was not bare. The walls were lined with shelves brimming with books, small statues, carvings and jars. The floor was covered with straw mats and large pillows. At the center was a fire pit, a hole in roof overhead.

"Welcome to my home," Simon said. "We have slightly more than an hour before the dragon men return."

"Why did they leave?" Mick asked. "They know we're here somewhere."

"They run to the harbor, because they see you running ahead of them."

"So, you do control minds," I said, thinking about the time Simon disappeared.

"I am not the only one, am I?" Simon stood. "We should leave."

"What do you mean 'we'?" I asked.

"You're going to the volcano. I am going with you."

"We're not going anywhere near that volcano," Mick said. "We're traveling south."

"Then I will follow you to the south," Simon said. "But know this. We will go to the volcano."

"Why do you say this?" Zhong asked.

"There are times when I simply know things. When I do, I am never wrong."

CHAPTER THREE

We left Simon's home and headed south, alternating between walking quickly and running. I kept glancing over my shoulder to check for dragon men—and Simon. He kept a steady twenty feet behind us. He had tied his robe around his waist to free his long legs and kept up easily.

"You can join us, you know," I said.

"I know. This is something else I must do to prepare for my destiny."

Zhong stopped us. In the darkness ahead was another line of faint lights.

"More dragon men," Simon said from behind us. "They have come to join the others. As I told you, more arrive almost every day."

"So, they don't know we're here?" Mick asked.

"Most likely not," Simon said. "But I do not know for certain."

"We will go around them." Zhong started off at a brisk pace. The rest of us followed, running west to get out of their path.

Thirty minutes later, we made another abrupt halt. Panting hard, Mick and I dropped beside Zhong. Simon sat twenty feet away. Another line of bouncing lights had appeared to the west. I looked to the south, and the lights were larger and closer. They must have changed direction. Now we had dragon men coming at us from the west and the south.

"The dragon men to the south have changed direction," I said. "They're heading directly for us!"

"Somebody has to be watching us," Mick said.

I looked at him. "In the dark?"

"How else could they follow us?"

"We have no choice," Zhong said. "We must head north."

That would take us to the volcano, just as Simon predicted. I looked toward it. We were closer to it than we had been in the town, and I had to tilt my head back to see its peak. It actually had two peaks and a red glow nestled between them.

I looked back at Simon, and he shrugged.

Zhong stood. "Come."

The four of us ran straight toward the volcano.

The air was hot long before the sun rose above the eastern horizon. We were running across an arid plain with scattered grasses and trees. Ahead of us was the gray and the green of a jungle at the base of the volcano. The volcanic ash cloud filled the sky.

Ash covered everything, including Zhong, Mick and me. The sweat off our brows made streaks down our gray faces. Simon and his clothes were again untouched by the ash.

I glanced behind me, like I did frequently. Each time I looked, I was shocked and troubled by how rapidly the dragon men were closing the distance between us. Now I could make out the individual men.

That was when I saw them: three black birds circling high above our heads. At first, I thought they were vultures, but then I recognized the shape. Crows. Their presence gave away our location in the daylight, but didn't explain how the dragon men had followed us during the night.

"There's crows above us," I said, panting.

"So, you were right, Mick," Simon said. "Someone is watching us."

"I meant people," Mick huffed.

"Those are not normal crows," Simon said.

By noon, I couldn't take another step, even with the dragon men closing in. I collapsed to the ground. Zhong and Mick dropped beside me. Simon sat twenty feet behind us. I looked around. The crows were still circling overhead. The two groups of dragon men had come together to form a solid line from south to west. They were close enough we could faintly hear their chanting.

"There!" Simon pointed at the jungle.

A man wearing a long white robe stood at the edge of the forest. I couldn't make out his face, but he was beardless, with long blond hair down to his shoulders.

"I know him!" Simon said. He jumped to his feet and ran toward the man.

We leapt up and ran after Simon. Zhong maintained the twenty-foot separation, but Mick and I lagged behind.

The man was motionless, until we were four hundred yards away. Then he stepped into the jungle and disappeared.

Simon was the first to reach the jungle. He plunged into the exact spot where the man had entered. Zhong and then Mick and I followed him inside, the crows shrieking overhead.

As soon as we entered the jungle, the sounds of the crows became muted, and the air became muggy and hot. A high, thick canopy of trees blocked out the sun and created a perpetual dusk. Unlike everywhere else, the amount of ash coating the floor and plants was scant.

We moved straight ahead, shoving vines and large leaves out of our way. We stepped onto a narrow path and saw Simon a hundred feet ahead of us. He waited until we were twenty feet away before leading us along the path at a fast walk. He kept looking right and left, even though we couldn't see farther than three feet on either side. We only slowed down when we had to push through dense plants or climb over fallen trees.

The faint chants of the dragon men grew suddenly louder, as they entered the jungle. Their voices mixed with the clumping and crashing of bodies rushing through the trees. The thought of a machete in the back kept Mick and me moving.

Then the sounds of the dragon men became fainter. I don't know how they lost our trail, but they did. When we could no longer hear them, Zhong turned to Simon. "We must rest."

Simon halted, and we sat where we were, with Mick and I dropping flat on the path.

Except for our noisy breathing, the jungle was silent. But after several minutes, the calls of birds, the cries of monkeys and the shuffling of life on the jungle floor returned. Mick passed the water bag to Zhong and me. Simon drank from his own bag.

I looked at him. "Did you ever see him, Simon?"

Simon shook his head. "No."

"Who was he?" Mick asked.

"I do not know."

Mick raised his eyebrows. "Didn't you say you knew him?"

"When I saw him, I had the strongest memory of his face looking down at me."

"We couldn't see his face," I said.

"I know," Simon said. "But it was him. He was protecting me."

"From what?" Mick asked.

"That is something else I do not know."

Mick sat up. "It's strange how the dragon men lost us."

"Simon's protector brought us to this path," Zhong said. "I suspect he also led the dragon men away."

I turned to Simon. "Is he protecting us?"

"All I know about the man is what I told you. But I believe Zhong is correct."

Zhong stood. "The dragon men will not remain lost. We must continue."

Simon stepped off the path until we had passed. Then he resumed his position twenty feet behind us. We followed the path, again moving at a rapid pace.

It was two hours later before we took another rest. I was lying on the path, enjoying not moving, when Zhong brushed my shoulder. I jumped up as something dark brown and the size of a hand scurried into the plants.

I shuddered. "What was that?"

"A spider."

"*That* was a spider?"

"The people call it Khabu," Simon said. "Its bite kills in ten minutes."

Mick sprang to his feet and brushed his clothes. "Anything else we need to worry about?"

"Snakes," Simon said. "The bite of the mambo kills in seconds."

"How do we keep from being bitten?" I asked, also checking myself for hidden predators.

"The only sure method is to remain outside the jungle."

"A little late for that," Mick grumbled.

We couldn't see the sun, but the deepening dusk told us it was setting. Zhong pushed off the path and led us to a clearing inside the plants. Simon sat on one side, and we sat on the other. As the blackness grew complete, I tried not to think about the spiders and snakes moving through the dark, seeking their next meal.

I took the first watch while the others rested. I had just taken a drink and was retying the water bag when the ground shuddered. I froze. Then a hard shake threw me flat and never stopped. The darkness sprang alive with groans, cracks and crashing sounds. Something heavy and thick with leaves landed on my back. It knocked the air out of me and drove me to the ground. With the crushing weight, it seemed like forever before the quakes tapered off and the jungle became unnaturally still.

"Is everyone alright?" Zhong asked.

"I'm fine," Simon said.

"That probably caused another tsunami," Mick said, "but I'm okay."

"I can't move," I said. "There's something heavy on my back."

"Are you injured?" Zhong asked.

"I might have broken a rib. I'm lucky the ground's soft."

"Mick, you and I will move toward John's voice," Zhong said.

"If you need my help," Simon said. "I will do whatever is needed."

I heard rustling. Hands on both sides felt me and whatever was holding me down. "I'm right between you," I said.

"Mick, there is a large branch on John," Zhong said. "Take hold of it. When I say, you and I will lift. John, are you ready to slide out?"

"I've been ready."

"Now, Mick," Zhong said.

There were grunts, and then the pressure on my back eased. I wriggled forward. The limb holding me down scraped across my back.

"I'm out!"

The branch thumped down behind me. Something big was in front of me. I reached out and felt a gigantic tree trunk. If the tree had fallen a foot closer, I would have been crushed. I silently thanked Destiny or whatever power had saved my life.

Since no place in the jungle was safe from an earthquake, we remained where we were. We rested, but no one slept. Every few minutes, another minor quake reminded us that another major one could happen any second.

We broke camp while it was still pitch black. We pushed through the vegetation and back onto the path and then speed-walked toward the volcano.

It was noon when we hit a dead end. The path and the jungle both ended at a wall of blackened trees and plants. The wall was three times Mick's reach. The air was thick with ash, smoke and the stench of sulfur.

"What do we do now?" Mick asked

"Until the dragon men stop pursuing us," Zhong said, "we should continue away from them."

Simon nodded. "I agree."

"Is this something you know for certain?" I asked.

"No, that is my opinion."

"That means we're finding some way around this wall," Mick said.

Pushing through the jungle, we followed the wall for fifty yards in both directions. There was no opening.

"Now it looks like we're climbing a wall," Mick said.

We all reached up for branches to use as handholds. As usual, Simon did his climbing twenty feet away. The climb wasn't easy. We had to stop constantly to untangle our clothes and bags. Zhong, Mick and Simon reached the top ahead of me. They all froze and stared at something. When I reached the top, what they saw stopped me, too.

The wall of plants was at the edge of a vast plain of smoking black lava. The crust was laced with glowing red-orange cracks. Scattered over the lava and partially hidden in a fog of smoke were the blackened remains of trees with twisted branches. They looked like tortured souls frozen in agony. Hovering above it all was the volcano's peak, which glowed like a malevolent red eye. I had a strong sensation it was watching us.

"I've got a bad feeling about this," Mick said.

"We must go on," Simon replied. "If you turn back, two of you will die. I know this for certain."

There was nothing to discuss. We climbed down the other side. I jumped the last few feet and hit the crust with a loud thump. Heat seeped through the soles of my boots. To minimize the contact between our feet and the hot crust, we hiked quickly toward the volcano, constantly stepping over glowing red cracks. Like always, I periodically checked behind and above us. I never saw the dragon men or the crows, which was good, but my gut told me it wouldn't last.

It was past midnight when we found an area on the lava that was hot but didn't burn. We were not sure if we would find another, so we stopped to rest. Simon volunteered to take the first watch.

I had just fallen asleep when someone shook my shoulder. "Time for my watch?" I muttered.

"We are leaving," Zhong whispered. "Simon saw a torch."

I forced myself to stand. The glow from the lava in the cracks outlined the dark shapes of my three companions with a faint red light. I stared into the darkness toward the wall but saw nothing.

"I don't see it."

"It's gone," Simon said. "But it was there."

We trotted toward the volcano's glowing peak, our boots thumping on the crust. Zhong somehow avoided them, but Mick and I kept bumping into blackened trees that seemed to leap out of the darkness and smoke. Forced to keep my eyes on what was ahead, I rarely looked behind me and never saw anything when I did.

My companions' shadows were easier to see, which meant dawn was near. I had not checked behind me for a while and took a glance. A point of light flared and quickly spread out to become a long line of lights.

"I can see the dragon men!" I yelled.

"And they're using animals!" Mick shouted.

Without slowing, we all looked back. The torches were bouncing as the dragon men ran after us. Between them and us were a dozen large dark shadows with glowing blue eyes. They grew larger as I watched.

Zhong increased his pace and turned us abruptly to the right. He was taking us back to the wall. We had to get off the crust before the animals caught up to us. Climbing back over the wall was the only way to do that.

I glanced back again, and the animals and the dragon men had already adjusted their course to follow us. I knew the reason. I looked up, and there they were—three black spots soaring above us.

"Simon, do you have your powder?" Zhong called back.

Simon was maintaining his twenty feet behind us. "Yes!" he said. "A pocket full."

"Everyone, be ready to stop," Zhong said. "Simon, when the animals are within range, throw the powder at them."

After running another fifty yards, Zhong came to a sudden halt. "Stop!"

We stopped and pulled out our knives. Simon put his hand in his pocket and faced the animals. They howled as they closed on their prey. They were almost to Simon when they stopped suddenly and lowered their heads. They growled and paced back and forth, as if uncertain what to do.

There was enough light, and they were close enough for me to recognize their shapes. They were jackals, but unlike any jackal I had ever seen. They were four times the size of a normal jackal and solid black with glowing blue eyes.

"Cover your eyes!" Simon shouted as his arm swept forward.

I threw a hand over my face. There was a loud boom, and a white light flashed between my fingers.

The jackals howled and yelped as the sparkling cloud engulfed them.

"Run!" Zhong yelled.

We had only gone a hundred yards when the jackals bayed and charged around the cloud. They split up to give Simon wide birth and run after the three of us.

"Keep running! Cover your eyes!" Simon shouted. He threw the powder at the jackals on both sides. There were two booms, two flashes of light, and more yelping and howling.

The wall was straight ahead. Simon used the powder three more times before we reached the wall and began to climb.

I was only halfway up when Zhong and Mick were almost to the top. The branches kept catching my shirt. Simon had reached the wall after me and was lower down when the jackals reached us. They initially went after Simon, but then, like before, stopped abruptly. They ran back and forth, sniffing and whining. A jackal turned away from Simon and leapt up at me. He clamped his jaws onto my right boot and began twisting and jerking me down. The branches I held broke. I began to fall, but then a hand grabbed my wrist.

"John, release the boot!" Zhong shouted. He had climbed down to help me.

With the jackal pulling, I wriggled my foot out of the boot. The jackal fell backwards, taking my boot with him. With Zhong pulling, I reached the top of the wall at the same time as Simon. The jackals jumped up at the wall repeatedly, growling and barking their frustration at having prey so close and being unable to reach it.

"Go on!" Simon shouted. "I have one last handful!"

Zhong, Mick and I were climbing down the other side of the wall when we heard another boom, and light flashed through the plants. The jackals wailed in pain.

As soon as our feet hit the ground, Zhong led us into the jungle. I looked up just before passing under the canopy of plants. The three crows were making tight circles above us and cawing angrily.

We crashed blindly through yellowed vegetation. I did my best to not slow down and ignored the pain of the sticks, roots and thorns stabbing and bruising my shoeless foot. The sounds of the jackals and crows grew fainter as we got farther from the wall.

We broke out of the plants onto a well-used path. Zhong called a halt to let us catch our breath. I collapsed and began pulling the thorns from my battered foot. Simon rested his usual twenty feet away. The volcano was partly visible through the trees overhead. There was no way to tell if we were on our original path or a different one.

"I know I'm slowing us down," I said, panting and picking at my foot.

"You're doing your best," Mick puffed. "Can't ask for more than that."

Zhong poured the water from his water bag into Mick's. He handed the empty bag to me. "This will be your shoe."

I slipped my foot into the leather bag and tied the straps around my ankle. Then I walked around to test it. The bag was loose and flopped on my foot, but it made walking bearable. "Thank you, Zhong. Which way do we go now?"

"We follow the path toward the volcano," Simon said

"Are we going to climb the volcano?" Mick asked.

"I do not know if we will actually climb it," Simon replied, "But if we go in any other direction, the dragon men will find us. Two of you will die."

"Is this more of your special knowledge?" Mick asked.

Simon nodded. Zhong stood. "We should continue."

Since Destiny had given us a single choice, we took it. Alternating between running and fast walking, we followed the path and were soon ascending the side of the volcano.

As we climbed the volcano, the path grew steeper, and the stench of sulfur became stronger. Our pace slowed to a trudging gait. The yellowed plants became increasingly scarce, until the ground was bare. I continued to glance up and behind us. I never saw the crows or anyone or anything following us. My gut said it would not last.

After hiking for several hours, we saw something on the path ahead. At first, I thought it was another burned tree without leaves. When we were close enough to see it clearly, we were shocked.

A man's body had been tied to a pole with the arms above his head. His body was covered with ash, and the swarming flies gave off a sickening buzz. The man's head was bent back, and his mouth hung open, as if he had died screaming. A large black crow stood on one shoulder and pecked at the holes where the man's eyes had been. In the center of the man's chest was a large black cavity.

"Simon!" I said. "The head from your smoke trick!"

"Now I understand what it is," Simon said from behind us. "It's a warning to turn back."

"I thought this was the safe way," Mick said.

"What I said was, if we went in another direction, two of you would die. I know nothing about this direction."

"The man has shoes, John," Zhong said, pointing at his feet.

I looked and saw crude leather sandals on the dead man's feet. Zhong removed a sandal and offered it to me.

I hesitated. "You want me to wear a dead man's shoe?"

"Yes." Zhong pointed at my foot. "Your bag has holes."

I knew he was right. I removed the bag and reluctantly placed the sandal on my foot. I walked around to try it. It was too large, but walking was easier, and it protected my foot.

"That is better," I admitted. "Good idea, Zhong.

Ignoring the dead man's warning, we resumed hiking up the path.

The sun dropped behind the volcano as we crossed a manmade ledge on the side of the volcano. Countless chisel marks covered the black stone surface and the adjacent wall. The edge overlooked a drop of several thousand feet. Below us was the jungle with a mixture of grays and greens. To the south was the plain of black lava. To the north was a massive body of water, the Bay of Tadjouri.

The ledge passed around an outcropping in the volcano and ended at a statue thirty feet tall. It was a man carved from the black volcanic rock. He had a short beard, hair down to his shoulders and a long flowing robe. He was sitting on a throne, bent forward with his chin resting on his right fist. In the deepening dusk, his face looked as if he had judged the world and found it lacking.

Beneath the throne was a dragon, its head and neck extending out from the right side and its tail twisting out on the left. Like Simon, the statue was without a trace of the ash that covered everything else. Something about the statue's face was strongly familiar, but that made no sense. I knew I had never seen the man before.

"Do you know who this is?" I asked Simon.

"He is the prophet of the dragon men."

"You've seen him before?" Mick asked.

"No, but I know he is the prophet."

Zhong walked into a high cleft in the stone alongside the statue. "This is the way forward." He bent down and picked something up, rubbing it between his fingers. "This is not volcanic ash. This is ash from a torch. The dragon men have come through recently. We must be alert—and silent."

With Zhong leading, we entered the cleft. We were on a tight path at the bottom of a narrow gorge. After hiking for ten minutes, the gorge widened, and the path changed to a steep ascent. We were forced back into a slow upward trudge.

We continued long after it was too dark to see. Zhong led, with Mick holding Zhong's shirt and me holding Mick's. Simon remained twenty feet behind us and managed the darkness on his own. We never spoke, but silence was impossible. The sulfur stench grew stronger, and the ash in the air became thicker. Our eyes and lungs burned, and everyone coughed.

Two hours into the steep climb, Simon whispered, "Dragon men!"

We halted and looked back. Behind and below us was a long snaking line of torches, at least a hundred of them.

"We must get off the path," Zhong said quietly. "Climb the wall to your right!"

Easier said than done. The wall was covered with small, loose rocks. There was nothing to grab that didn't move, and we slipped with every step. After climbing for a half hour, Zhong held up his hand. "Stop."

We heard faint angry talking that grew louder. The long line of torches soon passed below us. I was shocked to see they were less than sixty yards away. With the time and effort it took to climb the wall, I was sure we'd be higher up. We all struggled to keep from coughing and revealing our presence.

When we could no longer hear the dragon men or see their torches," Zhong spoke softly, "We must let them get as far ahead as possible. We can use the time to rest. I will take the first watch."

We tried to sleep when we rested, but no one could. The coughing and the burning in our eyes and lungs made it impossible.

CHAPTER FOUR

The ground heaved upwards beneath me and threw me sideways. Suddenly, I was sliding and rolling down the wall in total darkness. When I finally slowed to a stop, I remained flat.

"Is anyone injured?" Zhong whispered from somewhere above me.

We all confirmed we were fine.

"Continue to the bottom," Zhong said. "We will meet there."

I slid down the wall to the bottom. I heard the others sliding on both sides of me.

"Come to my voice," Zhong whispered when I reached the bottom.

I walked toward his voice and reached out, feeling someone's chest. "Is that you, Zhong?"

"Yes. Hold onto Mick's shirt, like we did before. Mick, hold onto me."

I felt Mick slide around me. I grabbed his shirt.

"Follow me," Zhong said. "Unless you must, no talking or sounds."

Hours later, we were all coughing and couldn't hold it back. Ash filled my nose and coated the inside of my mouth. The stench of sulfur and the burning in my eyes and lungs was more intense than before. I now could hear a distant thunder that never stopped. The world slowly brightened to where I could barely see my arm but not my hand holding Mick's shirt. We were inside the volcanic cloud and close to the peak.

Suddenly, a hand clasped my mouth from behind. I heard grunts in front and behind me. I struggled to free myself but stopped when a knife bit into my neck. My hands were jerked behind me and tied roughly at the wrists. I heard angry shouting and talking all around me. Hands grabbed my arms and shoved me forward.

The dragon men who had passed us in the night had been waiting for us. How did they know we were there? It must have been our coughing. As hard as we tried to hold it in, we couldn't stop it completely.

We had hiked for at least another hour. The thunder was almost deafening. That was when I stepped into clear air and a hot wind. I took deep breaths to cleanse my lungs. After twenty more steps, I was pulled to an abrupt stop. I looked around. Dragon men with knives and spears were in a long line in front and behind me. Mick was two dragon men ahead of me. Like me, he was being held by a dragon man, and his hands were tied behind him. I couldn't see Zhong or Simon.

I looked down and then jerked back. I was a single step from going over a cliff. It overlooked the volcanic crater, with its two towering peaks. The floor of the crater was a mile straight down and a chaotic mix of steaming black-and-red lava. Passing through the middle was a snake-like river of red lava. It flowed out from the base of a huge black stone pyramid on the right and poured through a gap in the crater wall to my left.

At the top of the pyramid was a large flat plateau. It was almost completely covered by a square black temple. Behind the pyramid and the temple was a massive churning column of gray-black smoke. It boiled up into the volcanic cloud. The thunder was from lightning bolts dancing along the smoke column and the cloud's undersurface.

The far wall on the opposite side of the crater was scarred with the shelves and squared vertical cliffs of a stone quarry. It was the source of the stone used to build the pyramid and the temple.

Hands pulled me back from the cliff and shoved me into the long line of dragon men. Mick was ten men ahead of me. Someone at the front shouted. The dragon men fell silent, and the line started forward. A knife jabbed my back. I ran to catch up with the man ahead of me. The line moved quickly down a steep path chiseled from the inside of the crater wall. With my hands tied, the buffeting wind and small rocks on the path, I struggled to keep from falling over the edge.

As we descended into the crater, the wind became a hot breeze. The path made a switchback, and I saw the entire line of dragon men for the first time. I still didn't see Zhong or Simon. If they had escaped, it meant they would save us. It could also mean they were dead, but I refused to consider that.

We reached the crater floor and followed a path of crushed black stone. The path wandered over the black lava and between and around the hot red lava. We were halfway across the crater floor when the path forked into two wide roads. The left fork snaked toward the stone quarry. We took the right fork toward the pyramid.

As we neared the pyramid, I realized it was far more massive than it appeared from above. The pyramid had been built with huge black stones, all precisely cut and squared. Every stone was covered with images of war, human sacrifice and men bowing to a dragon.

The road continued around the base of the pyramid to a steep flight of steps leading up to the plateau. Near the top of the steps were two dragon men in black feathered headdresses dragging a third man between them. The men walked onto the plateau and out of view.

We approached the bottom of the steps. That's when I saw a pile of bodies, each with a red hole in its chest. Movement at the top of the steps caught my eye. Something long rolled and bounced down the steps. As it came closer, I realized it was a man's body with a red hole in his chest. I couldn't look away until the body reached the bottom and tumbled onto a pile of bodies. I tore my eyes away from the horrors and focused on the ground before me.

The dragon men stopped in front of a long black wall twenty feet high and fifty yards wide. The wall was made of solid black rock, except for a large wooden door. A dragon man unlocked the door and pulled it open. Mick and I were pulled from the line. The ropes tying our wrists were cut, and we were shoved inside. We landed on people lying just inside the door, who moaned. The door slammed shut.

Mick and I were surrounded by walls that formed a square open to the sky. The pyramid and its steps loomed above us. The ground was packed with slumped, motionless men, women and children. It was a holding pen for workers and human sacrifices. The sulfur smell and the stench of human waste, sweat and vomit made a nauseating mix.

Mick said something, but I couldn't make out the words. The thunder from overhead made it difficult to hear. Mick put his mouth to my ear. "We need to get away from here!" He pointed to the wall farthest from the door.

I nodded.

Stepping between the prisoners as best we could, we picked our way to the wall. We squeezed in between the prisoners and the wall. It gave just enough space to sit without moving.

Something fluttered above me. I looked up and saw three crows on the wall with their heads turned sideways for a better look.

I tapped Mick's shoulder and pointed. Mick glanced up and shook his head.

I leaned close to his ear. "What happened to Zhong and Simon?"

Mick shrugged. "I don't know. Zhong disappeared when they took us!"

We settled back against the wall, powerless to do anything but wait for whatever came next. I wanted the next thing to be Zhong and Simon coming to rescue us. I refused to think about the other possibility.

The door opened, and two dragon men in black feathered headdresses grabbed a man near the door. They dragged him outside, and the door shut with a bang. Unfortunately, our spot gave us an excellent view of the pyramid steps. When the dragon men and their prisoner came into view, I lowered my head and closed my eyes against the horror to come.

Once each hour, the prison door opened, and two dragon men in headdresses entered. It continued through the night with the dragon men holding torches. Each time, I felt a surge of fear that they were coming for Mick or me. Each time, the dragon men picked their next victim from near the door. The dragon men never looked in our direction, but the crows that I knew were watching us in the dark made it clear we were not forgotten

———◄✖►———

At the first light of dawn, the door opened, as usual, but this time, five dragon men with black headdresses entered. Only one man carried a torch, and he led the others straight toward us. They were oblivious to the people they stepped on and their groans of pain. The fact it was happening meant Zhong was dead. If he were alive, Zhong would have already saved us.

The man with the torch held it close to our faces and nodded to the others. Two men grabbed Mick, and two men grabbed me by our arms. They pulled us to our feet and tied our hands behind our backs. The dragon man with the torch led us back to the door.

When we reached the pyramid steps, I decided to make killing us as difficult as possible. I pretended to pass out and let my body sag and my head drop. The dragon men struggled to carry my dead weight. I made things harder by catching every step with my feet. Mick saw what I was doing and slumped down to do the same.

After struggling up ten steps, the dragon men dropped us and began hitting and kicking us. The pain from the blows made us grunt, but we kept acting as if we were unconscious. I heard an angry shout from above. The dragon men grumbled, gripped our arms and resumed hauling us up the stairs.

Despite our efforts, we reached the plateau much quicker than I hoped. The roars of the smoke column and the thunder were so loud they hurt my ears. The dragon men dragged us into the temple and between rows of black stone columns toward a flickering orange glow. As we moved away from the entrance, the roars of the smoke pillar and the thunder diminished to loud rumbles.

We entered a large open space with flickering oil lamps on wrought-iron stands. The columns surrounding the space were filled with the same carved images of war, death and dragon worship covering the sides of the pyramid. The smoky, sulfurous air had a strong stench of burned flesh that made me gag.

In the center of the space was the statue of a huge red dragon. Mick and I were lifted into standing positions facing the statue. The dragon was upright with a massive head bending down from the ceiling to accept its offerings. It was red with black accents to its scales and black spikes along its spine and tail. Its open jaws bristled with teeth. In front of the dragon was a black stone altar with the black and brown of old and recent blood. To the left of the altar was a wide copper bowl on a stone pedestal. Inside the bowl were red-hot coals and smoking black hunks, the burnt remains of human hearts.

A tall, thin man in a flowing black robe and a black-feathered headpiece emerged from the darkness. Massive black animals with blue eyes, one on each side, moved with him, as if fused to his hips. They were jackals, like the ones that had pursued us across the plain.

The man stopped and studied us with dark, intense eyes and a smirk on his lips. I recognized him immediately. His face was the face of the statue at the entrance to the valley. The man was the dragon men's prophet. A feature of the man missing from the statue was the startling contrast between his white skin and his black eyes, black hair and black beard. As with the statue, I knew the face, even though that was impossible.

The prophet shouted a command. Two dragon men with black headdresses emerged from the blackness leading a man between them. It was Simon. I was relieved to see him alive. He kept his eyes straight ahead and did not look at us. He was placed in a line with Mick and me.

The prophet stepped in front of Simon, the jackals pressed against his hips. Then I knew why I recognized his face. Simon had black skin and white hair. The prophet had white skin and black hair. Except for their coloring, their faces were the same. The two men were identical twins and exact opposites at the same time.

The prophet gestured to the temple with a sweep of his hand. "A glorious place to die, is it not, my brother?" Like Simon, the prophet spoke perfect English, with an African accent.

Simon did not respond.

"I have been instructing Simon in the important truths of our lives!" the prophet continued. "Truths like his destiny and mine. Truths I have always known but which were strangely unknown to Simon."

The prophet waited for a reply, but Simon remained silent.

"Feel free to hide in silence, Simon. All I need from you…is your death. And I do not need your cooperation to take it."

The prophet turned to Mick and me. "From all reports, you are as ignorant as my brother. Or are you aware that you are the reason our god awakens?"

Simon looked at us for the first time with a question in his eyes.

"Don't listen to him, Simon," Mick said. "He doesn't know what he's talking about."

The prophet narrowed his eyes. "I know everything, including the Pathrakotau, the god who sleeps, and your precious Sanctuary. Your Oriental friend and his people have never understood whose sanctuary it is. But they will!" The prophet laughed.

"You mean the Soul of the Beast?" I asked.

"Fool. You say the words, but you do not understand them. But do not worry. I will help you finish what you began."

The prophet turned and stepped up to the altar. The jackals did not follow but kept their position, their eyes on us. The prophet lifted a knife from the altar. He looked at Simon and then Mick and me while playing his fingers along the sharp edge.

"I was telling Simon how our parents worshipped Pathrakotau. He rewarded their faith by allowing our mother to bear his prophet. But after my birth, our mother's labor continued, and Simon was born. Our god, in his infinite wisdom, had provided the sacrifice to honor my birth. But our parents' faith failed. They took Simon and hid him in the jungle. The faithful searched but never found him. Our parents claimed he was stolen, but their disobedience was clear. They took Simon's place as my sacrifice.

"I grew up believing you had died, my brother. And then you began performing those silly magic tricks. I actually watched one of your little shows, from a distance. I recognized my face in yours. That is when I knew why Pathrakotau had spared your life. You were to be the final sacrifice in his temple."

"Interesting," Mick said." A god who can't make up his mind."

The prophet's face tightened, and he closed his eyes. The jackals growled. "Pathrakotau controls all," he said in a low voice. "His way is perfect!"

"I am the firstborn," Simon said, breaking his silence.

The prophet opened his eyes, and his face flashed anger. "You, my brother, are an afterbirth. Nothing more."

"We both know I am the firstborn. You are not legitimate."

"Enough!"

The prophet gestured at his men. They put their knees against our lower spines and pulled our arms to bend our backs. The dragon man with the torch went down the line, tearing open our shirts.

"I had intended to show mercy by first cutting your throats," the prophet said, "but that is something you do not deserve. You shall now receive my god's full blessing. I will first take your hearts. Then you will watch as I offer your gifts to Pathrakotau."

The prophet turned back to the altar. He lifted the knife with both hands to the dragon and began to chant. The jackals kept their eyes fixed on us. Out of the corner of my eye, I saw the dragon men around Simon collapse. Then the men behind Mick dropped to the floor, followed by the ones holding me. I felt a quick sawing motion on the rope around my wrists, and then my hands were free.

"Take a knife," Zhong whispered in my ear. "Prepare to attack the jackals."

I pulled a knife from a dragon man's belt and held it toward the jackals. I saw that Mick and Simon were also ready with their knives. The jackals never moved. The prophet continued chanting, strangely unaware of what had occurred.

Suddenly, Zhong appeared behind the jackals and sliced a knife across their hind legs. The animals yelped as their legs gave way. They swung around to bite him, but he was already gone. Simon, Mick and

I rushed forward and drove our knives into the jackals' chests. They howled and then collapsed.

The prophet whipped around, shock and confusion filling his face. He shouted a command and ran into the blackness at the back of the temple.

Zhong reappeared and grabbed a torch. "Follow me!"

We raced after the prophet and then stopped abruptly at the back wall. The prophet had disappeared.

"Through here!" Zhong said.

He darted behind a stone column. Mick and I followed and squeezed through a narrow, vertical opening. I was surprised when Simon came through and stood right behind me.

The torch showed that we were in a narrow tunnel. The air was as hot as an oven. The roar of the smoke column was painfully loud. Zhong reached down and gave each of us a handful of fresh torches. He put the remaining torches under his arm. "This way," he shouted. We ran to the right, with Simon at the rear, as usual, but now close behind me.

After thirty yards, the tunnel turned almost straight down with steps like a stone ladder. I stumbled several times, causing Simon to run into me. Minutes later, we heard the echoing shouts and clumping footsteps of the dragon men, followed by echoing bangs and the pings and clangs of bullets and spears hitting the walls around us.

When we reached the bottom of the steps, the tunnel continued to descend at a thirty-degree slope.

As we ran, the echoing sounds of the dragon men grew louder, and the hot air became more bearable.

We entered a cavern that was so large the walls were beyond the reach of the torchlight. Without hesitation, Zhong took us to the far side of the cavern and a wall with openings into three tunnels. He lit a new torch and threw the old one into a tunnel on our right. Holding the torch, he bypassed a large opening and led the way into a small tunnel. We had to crawl on all fours to get inside. The sounds of the dragon men faded as we went deeper into the tunnel. They became abruptly louder when they found and entered our tunnel.

After an hour of crawling, we reached a place where we could walk upright. The tunnel quickly dead-ended on a fork with three openings. Zhong took bags from behind a rock and handed one to each of us. He lit a new torch, threw the old one into the opening on the left, and then took us into the one in the middle. As we hurried through the tunnel, the sounds of the dragon men grew fainter and then louder when they found our next tunnel.

As we plunged deeper into the maze of tunnels, Zhong's pattern for leading us through them repeated itself. We would reach a fork in the tunnel or enter a cavern with multiple tunnel openings. Zhong would light a new torch, toss the nearly spent torch into a tunnel opening and then lead us into another tunnel without hesitation.

I couldn't understand how Zhong knew which tunnel to take next. Except for the opening sizes, the tunnels all looked the same to me. I kept reminding myself that Zhong had saved our lives many times and had earned my complete trust, but I couldn't stop a growing fear that we were hopelessly lost.

I was staggering from exhaustion when we entered another cavern. It had a low ceiling and walls beyond the reach of the torch. Despite hours of constant hiking, the echoing sounds of the dragon men made it clear they were still behind us.

Zhong deviated from the pattern for the first time. He stopped us partway across the cavern and pointed to the floor. "John," he whispered, "stand here."

I stood on the indicated spot. Zhong turned me to face a certain direction. He handed me the flickering old torch and took my new ones. "Do not move," he whispered.

Zhong stood with his back against mine and took two steps. "Mick, Simon, when I am ready, hand the bags and torches to me."

"Where will you be?" Mick asked.

I looked over my shoulder to see what happened next. Zhong leaped up and grabbed both sides of a hole in the ceiling. He twisted and swung his legs into the opening and then pulled himself inside. His hand reached down. Mick and Simon passed the bags and the torches to him, and Zhong quickly pulled them inside.

"First you, Simon, then Mick," Zhong whispered and then lowered his hand again. "Jump with your arms straight up. Grab the sides. I will help pull you up."

Simon and Mick took turns lifting their arms, jumping and grasping the edges of the hole. They wiggled their way up, with Zhong lifting them by their wrists. I was alone in the cavern, the echoing shouts and steps of the dragon men making me nervous.

"John, do exactly as I say," Zhong whispered. "Look forward. Take ten normal steps in a straight line."

I took the ten steps and saw a tunnel opening behind a large rock on my left.

"Throw the torch inside."

I threw it into the tunnel as far as I could. Now I was in complete blackness. The sounds of the dragon men were getting closer.

"I don't like this!" I whispered.

"Shh..." Zhong said. "Without leaving that spot, rotate exactly one hundred and eighty degrees."

Turning in total darkness without moving off a spot was harder than I expected. "I did it. Now what?"

"Take twelve normal steps in a straight line."

I took twelve steps. In the darkness, I didn't know if they were the same distance or straight. "I'm here," I said, hoping that was true.

"Lift up your arms," Zhong said from above me. "Now jump."

I jumped. My fingers banged into the stone ceiling, and I landed with a loud clomp. The dragon men heard me, because there was an outburst of echoing shouts, and their footsteps sped up.

"Try again," Zhong whispered. "Arms up. Jump."

I jumped. My hands hit the ceiling again, and I landed with an even louder thump. Panic twisted my gut into a knot. "I don't know where you are!" I said, my voice shaking.

I heard a scraping sound. Red sparks fell from above me and to the left. I scooted beneath them.

"I'm under you now!"

"Jump."

I jumped, and this time a hand gripped my left wrist. Zhong pulled, and I climbed with my free hand. Once inside the tunnel, breathing was a lot easier. I raised my head and banged it on the ceiling.

"Make no sound," Zhong whispered. He placed a bag and torches in my hands. "Follow me. Do not stop until I tap your arm."

I moved blindly in a low crouch. Though doing my best not to make a sound, I kept making scraping noises. Occasionally, I bumped into Zhong who I could not see.

Suddenly, the shouting and clomping of the dragon men was in the cavern and close to our tunnel. I felt a touch on my shoulder. I stopped and sat with my back to the wall and looked back. The light of torches came through the opening into our tunnel and flickered on the wall. The opening was only twenty yards away, which was disturbing. I was sure I had crawled farther than that.

A head and a torch popped through the opening. The dragon man extended the torch in my direction. I fought the impulse to crawl away and pushed my body against the wall. I heard excited shouts below us, and then the head and the torch dropped out of sight. The sounds of the dragon men faded away as they entered the tunnel, where I had thrown the torch.

We remained silent and motionless long after we could no longer hear the dragon men. A tap on my shoulder surprised me. I picked up my bag and my torches and followed as quietly as I could.

After an hour of crawling through inky blackness, we entered a space, where we could stand. The air was warmer than in the narrow tunnel, and the smell of sulfur was stronger. I heard a scraping sound, and red sparks became a small flame spreading over the head of a torch. The torchlight revealed another large cavern. Carrying the torch, Zhong hurried quietly across the floor with Mick, Simon and I in a line behind him.

Mick stopped suddenly. "Zhong, what's that?" He pointed to a dark shape on the floor.

Zhong moved the torch closer. The light revealed the shriveled corpse of a man with a bare chest and tattered pants. He did not have a dragon tattoo.

"An escaped captive," Simon said quietly. "I do not see any evidence of injury."

"Then how did he die?" I asked.

"I see no supplies," Zhong said. "He may have been weakened by starvation before attempting his escape."

Mick and I didn't say anything, but we were thinking the same thing. A dead man on the path we were using to escape the volcano was a bad sign.

Zhong led us away from the corpse to the far side of the cavern. He stopped outside a tunnel opening and drove the torch into a crack. "We have escaped the dragon men," he whispered. "We can rest and speak. As a precaution, we should speak quietly."

Simon sat inside our small circle for the first time. Mick passed around the water bag, and I passed out the bread, Simon took his share, as if he always ate with us.

"No offense, Simon," I said, "but why are you sitting with us?"

"My fast and preparation ended when the dragon men grabbed me and dragged me into the temple."

"I've been waiting to thank you, Zhong, for saving us," Mick said. "Even if you did cut it a little close."

"Where did you go?" I asked.

"I did not know the dragon men were there until they attacked," Zhong said. "The prophet must have blocked my awareness of them. I could not see them in the cloud, but there were too many to attempt a rescue. I remained close by until I knew their intentions. I then left to plan our escape."

Zhong paused. "We should have known the Pathrakotau was not just a diamond. For centuries, men have searched for it, drawn by the myth that it gives immortality and invisibility to its possessor. I know now they were called by its evil, an evil to which we were blinded.

"No offense, Zhong," Mick said, gesturing toward the tunnel, "but you're sure this is the way out of the volcano?"

"As certain as I can be. While you were held captive, I found three routes of escape through the volcano. One is the main route. It is in constant use. We are following the least-used route. I traced it to where we sit."

"So, you haven't followed these tunnels to their end?" Mick asked.

"There was not enough time. You were about to be sacrificed"

"If you didn't make it to the end," I asked, "how did you know these are the right tunnels?"

Zhong picked up the torch and held it close to the opening. "Look down. Those are footprints in the gravel. There are scratch marks on both sides of the opening. These indicate frequent use."

Zhong always had excellent reasons for what he did. "Sorry I questioned you, Zhong," I said.

"It is best that you understand."

"If you still have doubts about this route," Simon said, "I will not die in this volcano. That means I will escape. If we stay together, we will all escape."

"Is this from your knowledge?" I asked.

"No. It is because of my destiny."

Zhong looked at him. "How do you know your destiny?"

"I have always known. I am to die as a sacrifice to a dragon."

"What kind of destiny is that?" Mick asked.

"Not the one I would choose. When you saw me in the temple, I believed my destiny had arrived. My magic left me the moment the dragon men grabbed me. After the prophet explained who I was, he told me that I was to be the final sacrifice to his dragon god. I believed his words. They matched what I knew to be true. Thinking I was about to die such a purposeless death crushed my spirit." Simon paused. "Then I heard Zhong's whisper in my ear. My magic instantly filled me. The relief was beyond words. I would not die in that temple."

Mick turned to Zhong. "What did you say?"

"I asked Simon to block the minds of the prophet and the jackals. I cannot control animals. The prophet is also beyond my control."

"Maybe you're not supposed to be a sacrifice," I said.

"The prophet was wrong about the timing and the place of my death," Simon said. "He was not wrong about the way I will die."

We sat and ate quietly in the dark, thinking about Simon's words and our desperate situation.

Simon broke the silence. "Since the prophet is your enemy and knows your secrets, perhaps your friend can know them as well. I'm curious about the Pathrakotau."

Zhong was quiet for a moment before speaking. "The Pathrakotau is the name for a blue diamond the size and shape of a bull. It exists in in a temple deep in the Himalayan Mountains, in a place called the Sanctuary. The Sanctuary is my home."

"Your people worship the Pathrakotau?"

"No. To us it is a diamond, nothing more. It has been with us since before our earliest myth. How it came to be with us, no one knows. No one has ever suspected its true nature."

What do you mean? Mick asked.

Zhong paused. "From what the prophet told us, the Pathrakotau is the crystalized, sleeping god of the dragon men. We should have known it was not just a diamond. For thousands of years, men have searched the Himalayas for the Pathrakotau or, as the world knows it, the Soul of the Beast. We thought they were drawn by the myth that the Soul would give them immortality and invisibility. I now believe they were called by its evil, an evil to which my people were blinded."

Simon nodded thoughtfully. "And what the prophet said about you awakening the Pathrakotau, is that also true?"

"Yes, but that wasn't our intention," I said. "We were returning two stolen diamonds to where they belonged. They had been cut from the Soul of the Beast. A monk placed them in their original locations, and a light inside the Soul began pulsing. A monk thought it might mean the destiny of the Soul had begun, but no one knew."

"It appears the diamonds were removed for a reason," Simon said.

A sudden violent shaking threw us flat on the floor. Dust and rocks rained down. We had no choice but to stay down until the quake stopped. Once it did, we pushed up and out of the rocks and debris and coughed to clear our lungs. The torch had been buried, and everything was pitch black. I heard scraping sounds and red sparks as Zhong lit a torch. We dug through the rubble and found our bags and the unused torches.

"Come," Zhong said. "We must leave these tunnels."

We entered the tunnel opening and moved as quickly as possible. When we reached a fork in the tunnel with six openings, I could now see Zhong scanning the tunnel openings for signs of use.

As we continued through the tunnels, we found an increasing number of corpses. Each time we did, the flickering torchlight made them appear to jump from the darkness. I wanted to believe the bodies confirmed we were following the right route, but all they really did was feed my growing fear that we were lost.

CHAPTER FIVE

After hiking through endless tunnels for what seemed like days, we entered another large chamber, gripped with a strong sense of urgency. We were burning our last torch. Zhong checked the tunnel openings by following the wall to our right. We had just reached the fourth opening when Mick stopped.

"Oh, no." Gathered around the opening were six shriveled bodies. Two sat with their backs against the rock wall and their heads flopped to the side. The others were piled in front of the opening. As if to emphasize the desperation of our situation, the torch flame sputtered and then flared once before plunging us into darkness.

No one said a word. We just dropped to the floor where we stood. I didn't blame Zhong. I knew he had done everything possible to escape the volcano. If he couldn't do it, nobody could.

"Remember what I told you," Simon said. "I will not die in these tunnels."

Mick sighed. "Tell that to the corpses."

I heard the crunching of footsteps followed by a ripping noise.

"What's happening?" I asked.

"I am making a torch." Zhong said.

"With what?"

"The clothes on the bodies. I am tearing off strips and wrapping them around the torch."

I heard a scraping sound, followed by red sparks. A small blue flame appeared and then spread over the torch head.

Light! Even though it had been dark for only a few minutes, the relief at seeing my mates' faces was like a huge stone lifting off my chest.

"I didn't know clothes burned like that," Mick said.

"These clothes are saturated with sulfur," Zhong replied. "Take all the clothing off the bodies."

We tore off every stitch of clothing and packed it into our bags. Without discussion, we resumed our search for the next tunnel, slowing only when Zhong paused to study the openings.

"Here," Zhong said at last. We entered the next tunnel.

The time we had left to escape the volcano was running out. The cloth on the torches burned too quickly, and corpses to tear more clothing from had become rare. To make the situation worse, signs of prior tunnel use were increasingly harder to find, and Zhong needed more and more time to find the next tunnel.

Then the inevitable happened.

We entered a cavern with openings into six tunnels. The last corpses were four tunnels behind us, and we were burning the last of the corpse clothing. Zhong was examining the second opening when the last torch sputtered, and the flame winked out.

"I will try to burn a bag," Zhong said.

I heard a tearing sound, followed by scraping and red sparks. The sparks landed on the cloth and disappeared. Zhong struck the flint repeatedly, but the bag would not light.

"Try my shirt," Mick said.

I heard more ripping and scraping, followed by sparks. The shirt would not burn either.

"Your shirt and the bag have not been exposed to the sulfurous air long enough to burn," Simon said.

There was a long silence before Zhong said, "There is one last option. I will use the flint for light. Form a line behind me."

By feel, we made a line behind Zhong—Mick, me and then Simon. Each of us held the shirt of the person in front. Zhong repeatedly struck the flint around the edges of the tunnel opening and over the gravel on the floor in front.

"This tunnel has not been used," he said and immediately began searching for the next one. We walked, holding the shirt ahead of us, our way illuminated by intermittent strikes of the flint. Our progress was slow, but at least we were moving. I knew Mick felt like I did about stopping. It was the first step to becoming another corpse.

Zhong led us along the wall, striking his flint and halting only to check one tunnel opening and then the next. He declared them both unused and not the route we sought. It was the tunnel after that when Zhong said the words we were desperate to hear. "This is the tunnel."

It was narrow, and we crawled inside, holding the pant leg of the person ahead of us.

The tunnel was unusually long. It was many hours before we reached another cavern. Zhong did not stop. He began striking his flint and following the wall to the right. He checked five tunnel openings that all appeared to be unused. When he struck the flint around the sixth opening, he stopped and sat still without saying a word. We dropped to the floor and waited in the blackness for him to explain.

"This is the tunnel we used to enter this cavern."

"How do you know?" Mick asked.

"Our footprints are all around the opening. I made an error when I chose this tunnel. We must return through this tunnel and find the correct one."

"Zhong, you don't make mistakes," I said.

"John's right," Mick said. "We followed the right tunnel. Going back won't change anything."

"Simon, what is your advice?" Zhong asked.

"I will die as a sacrifice to a dragon which means I will escape these tunnels. Since I will not leave you, we will all escape."

"Or you escape, and the three of us die in these bleeding tunnels," Mick said.

"I am not leaving you," Simon said. "Zhong, I suggest you recheck the tunnel openings in this cavern."

Without another word, Zhong resumed striking the flint and leading us along the wall.

After examining the new tunnels for a second time, Zhong stopped striking the flint and said nothing.

"You have to tell us sometime, Zhong," Mick said.

"There is no evidence that these tunnels were ever used."

"Maybe the problem is that flint," I said. "You can barely see with it."

"Whatever the problem, I cannot choose blindly," Zhong said.

We sat silently in the dark, unsure what to do. As I struggled to accept our predicament, I kept wondering if an escaped slave would someday follow our signs to that same dead end. Would he be shocked to see our dried-up corpses? Would he tear off our clothes and make torches? Would the torchlight allow him to find the way out?

It was a long time before I recognized a slightly gray spot in the otherwise inky blackness. I leaned forward for a better look, and the spot disappeared. I sat back and saw the spot again. I crawled toward the spot, an inch at a time. I adjusted my head after each movement to keep the spot in view.

"Who is moving?" Zhong asked.

"There's a gray spot in the darkness," I said. "I'm trying to find it."

The spot disappeared again. "It's gone! Did someone move?"

"I did," Mick said.

"Mick," Zhong said, "return to exactly where you were."

The spot reappeared.

"I see it!" I shouted, my voice echoing in the cavern.

I resumed crawling toward the spot. My shoulder was blocked by someone. "Who's that?"

"Simon."

"Simon, move away from me. Slowly."

When I no longer felt him, I resumed my slow crawl toward the spot. My forehead hit rock, and I groaned, more from surprise than pain. "Zhong, strike the flint. I need to see where I am."

The shower of sparks revealed a hint of a black opening with the gray inside. "This is the tunnel!"

"Do not move, John," Zhong said. "Let us come to you first."

I periodically said something to give the others a direction to follow. Minutes later, I felt a touch on my leg.

Zhong's voice came from next to me. "John, enter the tunnel."

The tunnel was narrow, and I had to crawl on my stomach to get inside. The walls scraped me on both sides, and I kept banging my head. As I moved forward, the spot became a more obvious gray.

"It's definitely a light!"

"We are in the tunnel behind you, John," Zhong replied.

It was impossible to know how far I had gone when the tunnel ended at a small gray hole. I pushed at the sides of the hole with my hands to widen it and felt earth and grass. When it was wide enough, I forced my way through. I was surprised by a fall of at least four feet. I hit a hard, flat surface with a painful thump. I lay motionless and exhausted on what I recognized was a warm lava crust. I opened my eyes and then shut them again. The light was blinding after what felt like days in total blackness. But time is meaningless in darkness, and I really had no idea how long we had been inside the tunnels.

I heard scratching noises above me, and I rolled to the side. There were three sets of thumps and grunts from my mates hitting the crust beside me.

"We made it!" Mick panted. "We're out of those bloody tunnels!"

We lay there for a long time without speaking, savoring our escape from the volcano.

Someone shook me.

"John, wake up!" It was Mick. "They already found us!"

I didn't have to ask who. I recognized the barking in the distance. I pushed myself to my feet. The light no longer blinded my eyes. We were on another plain of black crust with the burned remains of trees scattered across the surface. In the direction of the barking was a line of small black specks. For the jackals to find us so quickly, they must have had help. I looked up, and there they were. Three black crows soaring overhead.

"I hate those birds," I muttered.

"Don't we all," Mick said.

"Follow me!" Simon shouted and led us at a run away from the jackals.

As we ran, a roar ahead grew louder. Simon raised a hand for us to halt. We were at the edge of a cliff. The roaring came from a rushing river at the bottom of a deep ravine. The lava crust continued over the cliff and formed a black curtain that reached into the water.

"The Tadjoura River," Simon said, puffing for the first time that I had seen. "It empties into the bay."

I looked back. Two hundred yards away and closing fast were eight black bodies.

"Simon," Zhong said, "Do you have your powder?"

Simon felt in his pockets. "No."

The jackals howled as they began a final sprint to catch their prey. We knew why Simon had brought us there, and there was nothing to discuss. We sat on the cliff edge and pushed ourselves over.

I had begun to fall when a tearing pain in my left shoulder jerked me to a stop. My shoulder was clamped in a jackal's jaws. His pale blue eyes were inches from mine.

"Let go!" I yelled, trying to twist away.

The jackal growled and shook me. Jackals on both sides snapped their jaws at me. I whipped my free arm around and dug my fingers into the jackal's eyes. The animal wailed with an almost human scream. I plummeted and tumbled down the hard curtain of black lava.

WHOOSH.

I was suddenly immersed in warm brown water. My right side slammed into the rocky bottom before the current rushed me away. I collided with a rock that knocked the wind out of me. I was desperate for air, but I was tumbling under water and couldn't find the surface.

Suddenly, I was in the open air and falling. I took a quick breath before plunging back into the water. This time I did not hit the bottom. The water had slowed. I let the air in my lungs lift me to the surface. When I knew which way was up, I kicked and pulled myself to the surface. I took deep breaths and let the current carry me as I surveyed the situation.

A vertical wall soared on both sides, and a tall waterfall thundered behind me. Scattered bushes and grasses lined the river's rocky banks. I could not see my mates anywhere. I also did not see the jackals or the crows. Too exhausted to keep swimming, I worked my way to the shore. I crawled out of the water and crawled behind a large rock where, hopefully, the jackals and the crows would not see me.

I became aware of a rushing sound that reminded me where I was. I dragged myself out from behind the rock and looked around. I still didn't see the jackals, the crows, or my mates. With walls too steep to climb, the only way out of the ravine was to follow the river. That was where I would find my mates.

Forty yards downstream was a blackened tree. It was caught on rocks and bouncing up and down in the river. I decided to use it to float downstream. I waded into the water and let the current carry me to the tree. I pulled the branches free from the rocks. As the tree swung out into the river, I climbed up inside, passed my arms and legs through the branches and surrendered to my exhaustion.

I breathed in water and choked hard. I had fallen asleep and was too tangled in the branches to free myself and reach the surface. Fortunately, the tree rolled and lifted my head into the air. After I coughed out the water, I repositioned my arms and legs to make escape easier the next time. Then I let myself drift back to sleep.

I was awakened again, this time by the bouncing of the tree. The tree bounced all the time, and I decided to ignore it. Then I heard a growl. I turned my head to the right and stopped breathing. Six feet away and watching me through the branches was a yellow spotted leopard. The big cat snarled.

My first impulse was to swim for the shore, but leopards are good swimmers, and once on shore, I couldn't outrun him. My only hope was to stay in the tree and put more distance between the cat and me. I slowly untangled my arms and legs. The leopard tried to reach me with its claws and snarled when the branches held it back.

I slid into the water and grabbed a large branch farther from the leopard. I pulled against the current to reach the branch. When I came up for air, the cat was only three feet away. The current had pushed me in the wrong direction. I dropped back into the water. The leopard's claws swiped in front of my face, barely missing me.

WHOOSH.

The leopard was in the water beside me. The current turned the leopard and put its rear end in front of me. I broke off a branch and repeatedly stabbed the cat's rump. The leopard paddled away, trailing blood.

I surfaced for air inside the tree and looked around. Not seeing anything else, I pulled myself back into the branches. That's when I heard distant barking and scanned the sides of the ravine. I didn't see the jackals and let myself believe they had lost our trail. I relaxed and drifted back to sleep.

A throbbing pain in my left shoulder woke me from a troubled sleep. The tree was motionless except for a slow bobbing. I was in a large body of water covered with a layer of floating ash. The volcano's peak towered above me. I was in the Gulf of Tadjoura. The closest shore was a hundred yards away with jungle twenty yards from the water's edge. Anyone on the shore would see me easily. I had to reach the jungle and cover.

With the pain in my left shoulder, I couldn't swim far. Ten feet away was a thick branch I could use to stay afloat. I disentangled myself from the tree and slid into the water. Paddling with my right hand and kicking with both feet, I swam to the branch. Once I reached it, gritting my teeth, I draped my left arm over it. Then I kicked and pulled toward the shore.

When my feet touched bottom, three men stepped out of the jungle. I immediately pushed the branch back toward deeper water.

"John, stop!" someone said in a loud whisper.

I knew the voice. "Mick?"

"Shh…"

I looked back. Zhong and Mick were wading out to me. Simon was on the shore turning his head to watch in both directions.

"I thought I lost you," I whispered when they reached me.

"The feeling's mutual," Mick replied. He held me steady while Zhong lifted my left arm over the branch.

I couldn't stop a groan. "Easy," I said softly. "That's where I was bit."

They then pulled me toward shore.

"They're coming!" Simon said as they pulled me out of the water. He grabbed my legs, and the three of them quickly carried me into the jungle. We had just pushed inside the trees when I heard angry voices that grew louder. We watched through the leaves as more than a hundred chanting dragon men ran past us on the shore. After their voices faded away, Simon and Mick helped me stand, and we went deeper into the jungle.

They lowered me gently to the ground. Then Zhong pulled off my wet shirt and examined my shoulder. Everywhere he touched was painful.

"Where are the dragon men going?" I asked.

"We don't know," Mick said. "But something big's about to happen. A new group comes by every couple of hours, always heading the same way."

"This is badly infected," Zhong said, examining my shoulder. "We must treat it."

"I know something that will help," Simon said and disappeared into the jungle.

"Where did you go?" Mick asked me. "You were with us, and then you weren't."

"A jackal bit my shoulder and wouldn't let go."

"How did you escape?" Zhong asked.

"I gouged his eyes with my fingers."

Mick chuckled. "I like it."

"This will hurt," Zhong said.

I clenched my teeth as Zhong scraped the crusts off my wound with the end of a stick

"We didn't just leave you," Mick said. "We tried to find you. We searched all the way, went right up to the waterfall. After that, we floated down the river looking for you."

I groaned when Zhong squeezed out the pus. "I was behind a rock, hiding from the jackals and the crows."

Simon returned with a handful of green leaves. Zhong crushed them in his hand and packed them into the wound. He tore a strip of cloth from his shirt and wrapped it around my shoulder. "It will heal."

"Thank you, Zhong," I said and then looked at Mick and Simon. "Thanks to all of you."

"We've been discussing our next move," Mick said, "I want to find a boat and get away from this place. Simon wants to follow the dragon men. See what they're up to. I think it's just giving them another chance to kill us."

"We need to know what they're doing," Simon said.

"I'm with Mick on this," I said. "I want to get as far from dragon men as I can."

"Whatever is happening is something new," Simon said. "It is important for us to see this for ourselves."

"Are you speaking from your special knowledge?" Zhong asked.

"Yes."

"Well, when you put it like that," Mick said, "discussion's over. We're following the dragon men."

CHAPTER SIX

When the next group of dragon men was out of sight, we stepped onto the shore and followed them. We kept close to the plants to keep from revealing ourselves. The dragon men followed the shore for several miles before taking a wide well-beaten path into the jungle.

The path continued ten miles before it ended at a large open plain. It was the same plain we had crossed to escape the dragon men from the south. It had been empty then. Now it was filled with thousands of cooking fires surrounded by men. The dragon men were a hundred thousand strong.

"They have become an army," Simon whispered.

"An army for what?" Mick asked.

Simon pointed to a tall sprawling tent at the center of the campfires. "That is the tent of the prophet. Evil leaders always require luxuries they deny their men. The answer to your question is there."

Zhong gestured for us to follow him. He led us around the outermost campfire, where eight dragon men sat. Three men were shouting and angry. The others were either sleeping or cooking.

One of the angry men jumped up. I dodged to the side as he almost stomped into me. None of the men looked at us. I glanced at Zhong. He nodded to confirm he had made us invisible.

We continued toward the tent, passing between the dragon men and the campfires. Zhong motioned for us to sit by a campfire twenty yards from the tent. I sat with my face to the fire and studied the tent out of the corner of my eye. It had looked large from a distance, but up close, the tent was massive with multiple rooms. I recognized the prophet's loud voice coming from inside. I didn't understand what I heard, but the intensity in Simon's face showed he was listening.

There was movement at the tent entrance. I turned my head slightly for a better look, and my stomach jumped. Two large jackals stood motionless their blue eyes staring directly at us.

"The prophet knows we are here," Simon said softly.

"Do not move," Zhong whispered. He and Simon closed their eyes.

The dragon men around our campfire and the nearby fires leapt to their feet, shouting and thrusting knives, spears and guns into the air. They gave a loud shout and charged the jackals. Zhong motioned us to our feet. We ran back to the jungle as barks, yelps, shouts, screams and gunshots erupted behind us. I gritted my teeth against the pain in my shoulder.

The rest of the dragon men leapt to their feet. They ran around aimlessly, shouting, their weapons at ready, looking for an enemy to attack. Zhong and Simon blinded them to our presence, and we wove through them unseen.

We were at the edge of the campfires when a voice rose above the noise. All sounds stopped. I glanced back. The prophet was standing on something to elevate him above his men. He pointed at us. "*Hai tee! Kama hai tee!*"

The dragon men charged toward us. I heard gunshots and thuds as bullets hit the ground around us. It was a relief to push into the cover of the jungle, but we were in no less danger. We still had a hundred thousand dragon men chasing us with a single purpose.

To kill us.

We ran into Djibouti with the dragon men two hundred yards behind us. Simon led us through empty streets, alleys and collapsed houses. We emerged from an alley with the water and rock jetty straight ahead. The waterfront was empty except for two ships at the end of the jetty. The larger one was our crippled ship. The other was a small steamer with a slow thumping from the engine in the stern. A line of smoke rose from its small smokestack. The ship's wheel was on the forward deck in front of a small cabin.

Simon led us straight to the steamer. He and Zhong jumped aboard while Mick and I undid the ship's lines. Zhong went to the aft deck to adjust the steam engine. Simon was shouting something through the cabin's hatch.

After we freed the ship's lines, Mick and I threw them on the deck and then climbed aboard. We went flat on the deck and watched the town. The thumping of the steam engine sped up. Dark smoke billowed from the smokestack. The water behind the stern churned. Zhong came forward and took hold of the ship's wheel. We began to back away from the jetty.

The dragon men's yelling became louder as they poured around the huts onto the waterfront. BANG! BANG! BANG! Bullets thudded and clanged off the cabin and engine. Zhong and Simon dropped to the deck. Zhong continued steering by holding the bottom of the wheel.

We were ten feet out when two dragon men reached the end of the jetty and took a flying leap. They landed on the deck and threw themselves at us. I barely had time to grab the arm driving a knife into my face. It took both of my hands to block him, but the man was strong, and the blade moved closer.

The bullets thudding against the ship had become a barrage. The dragon man collapsed on top of me. A bullet from his own people had hit him. I pushed him off me and used him as a shield. His body jerked whenever a bullet hit. I pulled the knife from his clenched fist and looked at Mick. His dragon man was motionless, and he, too, was using the man's body for cover. Mick gave me a nod and lifted his new knife.

The gunfire kept coming until we were two hundred yards from the jetty. When it finally ceased, Zhong reversed the engine, turned the ship around and steered for open water. Mick and I shoved our dead dragon men into the water and sat with him and Simon.

"Whatever you heard, Simon," Mick said, "I hope it was worth it."

"Unfortunately, most of it was the prophet bragging that his army will be the greatest the world has ever known. Tomorrow, they march to the Valley of the Kings. That is all I heard."

"You've got to kidding," Mick said. "We almost died for that?"

"There was not enough time to hear more," Simon said. "The jackals cut our time short."

Mick and I sat quietly, letting our frustration and anger cool down. Zhong and Simon waited as we did.

Mick broke the silence. "So, what is this valley?"

"It's where the ancient Egyptians buried their pharaohs and nobles," I said. "It's to the north."

"Did the prophet mention his purpose for going there?" Zhong asked.

Simon shook his head. "No. That was all I heard."

"Well, the good news is we've got a ship," Mick said. "We know the dragon men are going north. And that means we sail south."

"We cannot start a trip by stealing a man's ship," Simon said. "We must have the captain's permission." He stood and knocked on the cabin hatch. "*Bwana, habaree ganee?*" No answer. "*Samahanee. Jina langu nee Simon.*"

After a few seconds, the hatch cracked open, and a voice from inside said, "*Jina?*"

Simon and the captain spoke for a long time. When they finished, Simon turned back to us. "I'd like to introduce our captain. His name is Paca. Before he does anything else, he wishes to examine his ship."

A thin African with a weathered face, balding gray hair and a thick gray beard stepped out of the cabin. He was barefoot with a torn shirt and pants. He gave us a quick look before walking around his ship, shaking his head. The glass in the cabin portholes was shattered. The cabin and the steam engine were riddled with dents. He paused for a closer look at his engine. He spoke to Simon who pointed to Zhong. Then he continued his inspection.

"What was that about?" Mick asked.

"He wanted to know who adjusted his engine," Simon said.

Paca finished examining his ship and then stood beside Simon. He spoke for several minutes. There was a back and forth discussion before Paca fell silent and waited for Simon to translate.

"Paca is angry with us," Simon said. "Djibouti was his home. Because of us, he is now an enemy of the dragon men. He can never return to his home."

"Probably not the best time to ask for a favor," Mick said.

"Paca wants to put us ashore, but to do that near Djibouti would be our death—and his. Paca is sailing north to Abu Sultan. I have asked him to put us ashore at Quseir. That will put us close to the Valley of the Kings. He has agreed, but we must act as his crew while we're on board. I have accepted for all of us."

"You did what?" Mick asked. "You tell him, you don't speak for the rest of us. And we're going south."

"I said it, because it's true," Simon said. "We are all going to the Valley of the Kings."

"More of your knowledge?" I asked.

"Yes"

"I don't care if this is your special knowledge," Mick said. "The prophet's not getting any more chances to kill us. Tell Paca we're sailing south. When we're out of danger, we'll go ashore, and he can go wherever he wants."

"That makes sense," I said. "What do you think, Zhong?"

"I prefer you and Mick choose."

Mick shook his head vigorously. "No, Zhong, this is a decision we make together."

Zhong paused to think. "Our destinies are connected to Simon's. I trust his knowledge. I believe we should follow him to the valley."

"That's one vote to go south, one to go north." Mick looked at me. "Guess what, John?"

"I have to decide?"

Mick smiled. "Must be your destiny."

I opened my mouth to say we should sail south but then stopped. I was overwhelmed by the strongest sense that if we didn't stay with Simon, something terrible would happen.

"John, please," Mick pleaded. "Just vote."

"All right. I say we go with Simon to the Valley of the Kings."

Mick shook his head. "Am I the only one who wants to live?"

I shrugged and held up my hands. "You told me to decide." Now that I had, I knew it was the right choice.

With nothing left to discuss, we introduced ourselves to Paca, pointing to our chests and said our names. Paca nodded and repeated our names. "Meek. Joan. Sung."

BOOM!

We swung our heads toward the blast. Mount Tadjoura was spewing streamers of red fire. Lines of red lava poured down the volcano's sides. I thought about the hundreds of captives trapped at the top. After all their suffering, they were being buried alive in hot lava. I silently asked Destiny to keep them from the pain and kill every dragon man in the volcano.

As we sailed north through the Red Sea, the volcanic cloud remained overhead, keeping us in constant dusk. Paca instructed Mick, Simon and me in how to function as the crew. He did this through demonstrations and verbal explanations translated by Simon. Whenever Paca needed to rest or check something on the ship, Zhong was the only one he allowed to steer.

We stayed out of sight of the western shore as much as possible. When we saw other boats, Paca would change course to avoid them and increase our speed. He did not want the dragon men to find us, and we all agreed with that.

On the morning of the third day after leaving Djibouti, we passed out from under the volcanic cloud. After being in the dim light for so long, the clear, bright sky felt strange. By noon, the ship's deck and surfaces had become too hot to touch. The insides of the ship's holds had turned into ovens. We had nowhere to sit or escape the heat. Paca, who was manning the wheel, spoke to Simon.

"Paca wants us to use a tarpaulin to create cover from the sun," Simon said. "The tarpaulin and the poles are inside the cabin."

"What're we waiting for?" Mick asked. He looked in the cabin and pulled out a linen tarpaulin with two poles wrapped inside. Following Paca's instructions, we unrolled the tarpaulin and tied two corners to the cabin roof. We tied the other corners to the poles and braced them upright with more line. Now we had shade and a place to sit out of the sun.

Even under the canvas, however, the heat was intense. Paca spoke to Simon again. "Paca says to fill the bucket and dump the water over our heads."

I was embarrassed that I hadn't thought of that. There was a bucket with a line tied to the handle. When we needed to refill the boiler, we tossed it into the sea and pulled it back, full of seawater. I tossed the bucket into the water and offered it to Paca. He smiled and poured it over his head.

Paca, Mick and I rested under the tarpaulin while Zhong manned the wheel.

Paca leaned out to see something and frowned. "Bad!"

Mick stuck his head out. "We've got company."

Standing on the cabin's roof, still as statues, were three large black crows. Each bird had its head turned to the side with a black eye watching our every move.

Mick and I reached for pieces of wood on the deck. Before we could cock our arms back to throw, the crows flapped up into the sky and settled into slow circles high above the ship.

"Too bad," I said, dropping the wood.

"Those are definitely not normal crows," Zhong said.

Simon nodded. "No, they are spies for the prophet. He uses them to hear and watch us."

"How can he see and hear us through a bird?" Mick asked.

"The prophet has a magic like me, only stronger. Unlike mine, his is always available and under his control. He uses it for many things I cannot do, including seeing through the eyes of crows, hearing through their ears."

"Could your magic kill the crows?" Mick asked.

"Everything is possible."

"Want to give it a try?" I asked.

"As I have told you, my magic acts when and how it chooses. At the moment, it chooses to do nothing."

The next morning, Paca angled the ship toward the western shore of the Red Sea. At first, all we saw was the green of grasses and palm trees. As we neared the shore, three mud brick huts came into view.

"That's Quseir?" I asked. "A little small to be on a chart."

"This is an oasis in a dry desert," Simon said. "The water makes Quseir important."

I looked up. The crows were still circling. Mick and I always had something in our pockets to throw. The birds must have known, as they remained high in the sky. We couldn't stop them from watching, but we had stopped them from listening. Mick and I considered that a partial victory.

Paca cut the engine, and the ship drifted up to a short jetty of piled rocks. We hit with a soft bump. Mick and I jumped off and tied the ship's lines to the rocks. The only visible life was a camel squatting and chewing its cud beside a hut. Beyond the palm trees and plants lining the shore were barren, rolling sand dunes. In the distance, shimmering in the heat, was a line of sand-colored hills.

Paca stepped off the boat and led us to a hut with a small, doorless entry. He stopped outside and shouted. An old, withered man, bent at the waist, shuffled out through the opening and stood erect. He wore a simple white tunic and a white head-cloth tied to his head with a brown cord. He looked up at the crows and frowned.

Paca bowed and spoke. The old man nodded and led us to the shade under the palm trees. He sat with his back against a trunk and gestured for us to join him. Two young women in white tunics emerged from another hut carrying pots and clay cups. They poured brown cloudy water into the cups and handed one to each of us. We drank while Paca and the old man spoke with each other, and Simon translated.

"Our host is Omar," Simon said. "He tells Paca that an army is coming from the south. He says they are a sea of locusts devouring everything in their path. They kill everyone who does not join them. Omar expects them to arrive here in two days.

He asks Paca if this army will join the one by the pyramids."

"There's another army?" I asked.

"Apparently so. Paca says we know nothing about the army to the north. He says the southern army's destination is the Valley of the Kings. He asks if Omar knows why they would go there."

Simon stopped translating to listen closely. Omar shook his head and said something. Paca spoke to Simon, who responded. Paca appeared to repeat Simon's words to Omar. Omar looked at Simon and then the three of us with concern. Omar and Paca began another discussion, which included Simon. The conversation stopped. Omar and Paca silently watched our faces.

"What has happened?" Zhong asked.

"Omar asked Paca for our destination," Simon said. "When Paca said we were going to the valley, Omar asked why we would go to the same place as the army. Paca said he didn't know. Omar asked me. I told him it was our destiny. Omar said we must be wrong about our destiny. We should leave now. Sail south while we can. Once the southern army arrives, the entire desert will be a very dangerous place."

"At last, someone else with common sense," Mick said.

"As you know, my friends," Simon said. "I must continue to the Valley of the Kings. But it is not too late for you to change your minds. Paca has agreed to take you south."

"Change our minds?" I said. "So, we're supposed to decide again?"

"Apparently so," Mick said. "My vote hasn't changed."

My sensible side still agreed with Mick and now Omar. Sailing south was the only option that made any sense. Deliberately staying in the sights of an army was crazy. But for reasons I could not explain, my commitment to staying with Simon was stronger than ever.

"Neither has mine," I said. "I still choose to stay with Simon."

Mick looked at Zhong "I assume your vote's the same."

"Yes. I am certain our destiny is to follow Simon."

"I'm glad we're staying together," Simon said. "Whatever is about to happen, we must face it together."

Mick sighed. "Sounds like more of your special knowledge."

"It is."

Simon started another discussion with Paca and Omar. When they stopped, Omar gave a shout. Four sleepy boys with uncovered heads and white tunics stumbled out of the farthest hut. Omar spoke, and then the boys ran into the desert. Omar and Paca put their backs against the palm tree and closed their eyes.

Simon turned to us. "Omar will provide what we need for our trip."

"Really?" I said. "Why would he do that? We have nothing to trade."

"We don't, but Paca does," Simon replied. "He has agreed to take Omar and his family south in exchange for camels and supplies. Omar was already preparing to leave, and this makes it easier. If he is here when the army arrives, they will take all that he has and kill him, his sons, his wives and his daughters."

Mick nodded at Omar. "If he's in such a hurry, why is he taking a nap?"

"He is not sleeping," Simon said. "He is waiting.

"For what?" Mick asked.

"See for yourself."

Women and children stepped through the trees carrying sacks in their arms and on their heads. They sat silently in a semicircle around Omar.

"This is Omar's family," Simon said.

"That was fast," Mick said.

"Survival in the desert demands it."

Another ten minutes passed, and the young men returned leading a train of five single-humped camels. Each animal was piled high with bags and bundles of firewood. The camels padded past us to the ship. Omar's family stood and followed Paca with their possessions. Paca stood, bowed to Omar, then returned to his ship to supervise the loading of his ship.

"Mick, John, please, go with Paca," Simon said. "You can speed things up. Zhong and I are to remain with Omar."

As Mick and I helped Paca stow everything in and on his ship, we watched Omar teach Zhong and Simon how to make the camels sit and stand. The camels sat by bending the knees of their front legs, dropping their haunches to the ground and then folding their front legs flat. To stand, the camels reversed the procedure.

Once the ship was loaded, Omar shouted. Mick and I followed Paca and Omar's family back to the shore. We sat in a circle with Simon in the center. A boy placed an armful of sticks before Simon before joining the others. The crows continued to soar above us, watching intently.

Simon stooped and arranged the wood into a small pyramid. He moved his hands in a circle over the wood, and it burst into a bright yellow flame. He took a handful of dirt from the ground and poured it onto the fire. The flame went out and was replaced by a thin column of smoke that rose straight up.

Simon chanted in a low, rhythmic voice, and the smoke began to thicken, sparkle and rotate. It spun faster and faster until it was a blur. Without moving my head, I watched the crows. They were circling closer to the ground. I pulled a stone from my pocket and waited for the opportunity to use it.

Simon stopped chanting. The spinning of the smoke slowed and revealed an African woman twirling on the tips of her toes with her hands at her sides. Every detail of her body and face was perfect, down to the individual lashes of her closed eyes.

When the rotation stopped, the woman's eyes burst open. Everyone sucked in their breath.

The woman closed her eyes again and began to sway. Her body moved in and out of curves to music that only she could hear. Her face said the music was beautiful beyond words. She reached forward with open hands and brought her hands to her face, as if scooping fragrance from the air. She wrapped her arms around her chest and tilted her head back.

The crows were sixty feet above us and slowly descending. I shifted my weight off the hand with the stone.

The woman bent slowly at the waist until her head almost touched the ground. She remained in that position for endless seconds. Suddenly, she straightened up and shot into the sky, becoming a flaming ball as she headed straight for the crows. The birds had only enough time to pull back their wings before the fireball hit them and exploded. The birds burst into flames and plummeted to ground, leaving trails of spiraling smoke. Their smoking bodies plopped on the ground at Simon's feet.

There was a stunned silence before everyone clapped and shouted. Simon smiled and bowed.

Mick grinned. "Now that's what I call magic!"

After we thanked and exchanged bows with Omar, the two boys holding his arms helped him onto the ship. Then we said our goodbyes to Paca. He spoke briefly to Simon before giving each of us a crushing hug, tears flowing from his eyes. Then he jumped onto his ship, started the engine and stepped behind the wheel. He waved as his ship backed away from the jetty.

I turned to Simon. "What did Paca say?"

"That we are now his family. If we ever need his help, we have only to ask."

With the dragon men army only two days away, we mounted the camels and rode into the desert. We went single file, with Zhong's camel in the lead, my camel next, then Mick's and finally Simon's. The reins of the supply camel were tied to Simon's saddle. Following Omar's instructions, Zhong led us west toward the hills. The sun reflecting off the sand made the hot air hotter than it already was. We were grateful for the white head-cloths Omar had given us for protection from the sun.

As the camels walked, they rocked back and forth and side to side. The motion made me queasy. I wished we were riding horses. I was in danger of embarrassing myself by getting seasick on land.

The sun was at its noonday peak when Zhong halted us beside a sand dune. "We stop here. Omar said, when possible, avoid riding under the midday sun."

We dismounted. To make shade, we staked one side of a canopy cloth into a sand dune and elevated the other side with two wooden poles. Before stepping underneath, I looked up. Three black specks circled above us.

"More crows," I said.

Zhong nodded. "They have been with us for miles."

Mick dropped next to Simon. "Any chance of the smoke lady coming back?"

He shook his head. "The magic never repeats itself. The smoke lady is gone forever. But the crows do not change anything. The prophet has known our destination from the moment we left the ship."

I took the water bag from Zhong. "What's our plan?"

"We continue west until we find a path," Zhong said. "The path will take us to the Nile River. From there we head north until we find a ferry to take us north. When we see hills on the far side of the Nile, we have arrived at the Valley of the Kings."

"Simon," Mick said, "any idea yet why we're going there?"

"No, but I know Zhong is correct. You are all destined to travel to the valley."

The sun was dropping behind the hills when we began to climb them. The terrain changed to a mixture of sand and hard ground. To take advantage of the cooler night air, we intended to ride through the night and into the next morning.

Something black fluttered over my head. I ducked. "Did anyone see that?"

"John!" Zhong shouted. "Ride to the left!"

I pulled the camel's reins hard to the left. More black things flew past, their wings buffeting my face. The black things became a thick swarm. My camel groaned and jerked to the right, throwing me to the ground. My head hit something hard with a spike of pain. Then everything went black.

Someone gently shook my shoulder.

"John." It was Zhong.

I opened my eyes to complete darkness, except for the stars overhead. I turned toward his voice, and a stab of pain made me groan.

"That answers the question," Zhong said. "You can't continue. We will camp here tonight."

I touched the right side of my head and found a tender mass. "I won't be the reason they catch us."

"John, you can't even turn your head," Mick said. "How're you going to ride a camel?"

My head hurt too much to argue. "What was that?"

"Bats," Simon said. "They come out at dusk. You were outside their cave when they did."

"You've got a knack for getting hurt by animals," Mick said.

"Go back to sleep, John," Zhong said. "We'll check you in the morning."

I felt another gentle shake of my shoulder. Everything was still black. The shadow of Zhong's face was above me.

"Before I wake the others, I need to know if you can ride. I will help you to sit."

Zhong lifted me by my arm. The movement made my head throb. I clenched my teeth to keep from crying out.

"It's better. I can ride," I said, not sure if that was true.

"It is still painful," Zhong said.

"It's nothing, Zhong. I'm ready to ride."

Zhong paused before letting my lie stand. "There is water and food beside you. I will wake the others."

It was dark when we urged the camels forward. The motion of my camel made my head worse, but I said nothing. However, when my camel stumbled and jerked my head, I couldn't hold back a grunt.

"We can rest if you need it," Zhong said.

"The camel made a funny move. It surprised me. That's all."

Because of me, the dragon men were a half day closer to catching us. I refused to be the reason for another delay.

The sun was above the horizon when we reached the summit of the mountain and started down the other side. The air was starting to warm up. The land ahead was more barren sand. Beyond the shimmer was the Nile River and a ferry to our appointment with Destiny.

CHAPTER SEVEN

I t was noon when we reached the Nile River. We rode north along its shore. After the lifeless desert, the green along the river was a refreshing change. We passed scattered brick huts and women performing chores while small children ran and played. Men in small boats with white sails cast their nets into the water. Everyone stopped to stare at us before resuming their activities. Unlike Omar, the people were oblivious to the coming storm. Their ignorance would not last long.

We halted the camels beside a large raft pulled onto the shore. The raft had been built with split tree trunks on whole trunks. It had a mast at one end and a large rudder on the other. We dismounted under the shade of a palm tree. We released the camels to drink from the river. An old woman emerged from a hut. She looked at us but said nothing.

"I will speak to her," Simon said.

He greeted the woman. They spoke for a long time, with Simon pointing to the north, the river and the three of us. He placed something in the old woman's hand. She looked at it before walking north along the shore.

Simon sat with us. He nodded his thanks when Zhong passed him dried dates and the water bag. "The woman's sons will take us to the Valley of the Kings," he said. "We are to rest here until they are ready."

"I assume they aren't doing this for free," I said.

Simon bit into a date. "No. Omar gave us a golden piece for the fee."

The old woman returned with two boys. One carried two long poles, and the other had his arms around a rolled-up sail. The boys went to the raft, and the woman returned to her hut without a word to us. The boys tied the sail to the mast and pushed the raft into the water. They used the poles to hold the raft against the shore and gestured for us to board.

We led the camels onto the raft and had them sit in the center. The boys poled us to the center of the river and into the current. The raft bobbed in the moving water, and the camels protested their uneasiness with loud moans.

Over two hours later, we spotted hills beyond the western shore. Omar had said the hills would mark the Valley of the Kings. I looked up. The crows were still circling overhead.

One boy dropped the sail and picked up a pole. The other angled the raft toward the shore with the rudder. When the raft touched the shore, the boy at the rudder grabbed the second pole. The boys held us against the shore with the poles and motioned for us to disembark.

Zhong, Mick and I led our camels off the raft. Simon handed each boy a coin before leading his camel ashore. The boys poled back out into the Nile and raised the sail.

Simon looked up. "Before we leave, there is something I should do."

We followed his gaze to the crows. They burst into flames and then spiraled down, trailing smoke until they plopped into the river.

"I was hoping to see the smoke woman again," Mick said. "But that will do. Thank you, Simon."

Simon smiled. "Thank the magic."

We rode straight for the hills. The camels were running at what was full speed for them and a trot for a horse. I was bounced in all directions at once. I gritted my teeth against the pain in my head, but it was finally too much to bear. I was about to ask Zhong if we could slow down when he pointed behind us. A low cloud covered the horizon to the south. It looked like a sandstorm, but I knew it wasn't.

"The prophet's army!" Zhong shouted. "They are eight hours behind us. Whatever we are to do in the valley, we must do it quickly."

I clenched my teeth harder and said nothing.

We rode to the top of the nearest hill and halted. Our camels moaned loudly at their abuse. Below us was a barren valley that snaked between sloping walls on both sides. The walls were covered with holes and piles of sand and dirt. The far end of the valley was hidden behind a bend and dominated by a tall hill shaped like a tiered pyramid. The valley did not look like a burial ground for pharaohs. It looked more like the gold fields of South Africa.

"Any idea yet why we're here?" Mick asked Simon.

"No, nothing," Simon said with disappointment in his voice.

"Why would they bury the pharaohs here?" I asked.

"To hide their burial sites," Simon replied. "Pharaohs and Egyptian nobility were buried with great treasures."

Mick shielded his eyes with his hand and scanned the valley. "With all the digging that's gone on, I doubt there's anything left to find."

"There has to be," Simon insisted.

"Come," Zhong said.

We urged the camels forward, but they refused to move. They were exhausted. We had no choice but to dismount and lead them by the reins. I took one last look behind us before we climbed down. The dust cloud was larger.

We descended to the valley floor and walked forward, looking at and into everything. Every hole was empty. We found nothing that we hadn't seen from the top of the hill.

We reached the bend in the valley and pulled the resisting camels around it. We were desperate for something to explain why we were there. That part of the valley ended four hundred yards away. It was covered with more empty holes and piles exactly like the first part, except for the tall pyramid-shaped hill at the end.

We stopped and stared quietly, trying to understand why we had traveled hundreds of miles and risked our lives for nothing. I mentally kicked myself for being so stupid. Why hadn't I voted with Mick?

Zhong broke our silence. "He is there."

Standing at the base of the pyramid-shaped hill was a man. He hadn't been there a second before, because if he had been, we would have seen him. He had long blond hair and wore a simple white robe. He was beardless, and that was the only feature of his face I could see. He was the man who had led us into the jungle.

We ran toward him, pulling the camels into a trot and ignoring their moans. The man turned and climbed the hill.

"Wait!" Simon shouted. "Don't leave!"

The man continued climbing without looking back. When he was halfway to the top of the hill, he stepped over an edge and out of sight.

We reached the hill and released the reins, leaving the camels to wander. We climbed as fast as we could to the place where the man had disappeared. It was a flat shelf covered with sand and rocks. The man was nowhere to been. We dropped to the ground, panting.

"He must've climbed to the top," Mick puffed.

"He led us here," Simon said. "The reason we came to this valley is here. We have to find it."

We pushed ourselves back onto our feet and staggered over the shelf, lifting rocks, digging with our hands and looking into crevices. After finding nothing, we came together again and collapsed. Unfortunately, the water bags were on the camels. I was desperate for water but too exhausted to climb down and fetch a bag.

"Where did the crows come from?" Mick asked.

I shielded my eyes and looked up. Hundreds of black birds swirled above us like a black cloud. The crows suddenly bunched together and flew in tight, rapid circles with loud, intense cawing.

"They see something," Zhong said. "We must go higher."

He began climbing the hill. The rest of us scrambled to catch up.

When we reached the top, we were a hundred yards above the shelf. We looked down, expecting to see whatever had excited the crows, but there was nothing but rocks and sand.

Then Mick pointed. "There it is!"

"Yes!" Simon said with relief.

Suddenly, the rocks below us came together in my vision. They formed the shape of a bull inside the jaws of a dragon,

"The Soul of the Beast," I said.

"We dig under the bull," Simon replied.

Mick looked at him. "Are you sure?"

"Yes." Simon led us at a sliding run back down the hill.

As we descended, I glanced at the dust cloud created by the dragon men army. It was bigger and closer than it should have been. The dragon men had to be running. How they could do it in this heat, I didn't know. More important than how was the fact they were just hours from reaching the valley.

Once we reached the shelf, the stones appeared to be scattered once again.

"So, which one's the bull?" Mick asked.

I shook my head as I looked at the rocks. "I can't tell one from another."

Zhong placed his hand on a rock. "This is the center of the bull. I kept my eyes on it as we came down."

"Thank you, Zhong," Simon said.

We began digging and pulling sand away from the rock with our hands. I was still dying of thirst. We all were, but we were too close to our goal to stop.

We had dug down three feet on all sides when Mick shouted, "I got something!"

We quickly joined Mick in pulling sand away from a hard, flat surface with a straight edge. Digging around the stone revealed a second flat stone to the side and deeper than the first. We dug further and found a third stone lower than the others.

"Steps," Zhong said.

We kept digging and exposed a six-step staircase. It ended at a flat stone that was three feet square. Each edge of the bottom stone had a cut-out in the middle.

"Handholds," Mick said. "Let's try and lift it."

We each grabbed one and prepared to lift

"Now!" Mick said.

We pulled with every ounce of our strength. The stone did not budge. We pulled again until our arms and shoulders burned, and still no movement. It wasn't until our seventh attempt that we heard a grating sound. The stone had moved a hair's breadth. We shook our arms and yanked again. We were rewarded this time with a hiss of escaping air. We wrinkled our noses at the faint odor of incense mixed with burnt flesh.

We kept pulling until we could slide the stone to the side. We lifted it on an edge and out of the way. We looked down into the square opening and complete blackness.

"I'll get a rope and a torch," Mick said, already running up the steps.

"And a water bag!" I shouted after him.

Simon reached inside the opening and felt around. "Lower me down."

"We should wait for the rope," Zhong said.

"We've all seen the dust cloud," Simon replied. "This cannot wait."

Simon lay on his abdomen and slid his legs into the opening. Zhong and I held his hands and lowered him into the darkness as far as we could reach.

"My feet aren't touching," Simon said.

"We're bringing you up," Zhong replied.

"No. Release me."

"Are you sure?" I asked.

"Yes."

Zhong and I opened our hands. Simon dropped into the darkness with a thud.

"I'm fine," Simon said. "It's another four-foot drop."

"Can you see anything?" I asked

"Just where the light comes in through the hole. There are carvings in the floor. Hmm...that's interesting."

"What is?" I asked.

"The carvings show men worshiping a dragon. This is not a pharaoh's tomb."

"It's a second temple," Zhong said.

"You're right," Simon replied. "We now know the prophet's purpose for coming here. I believe this place will show us why we are here."

Zhong was inside holding the torch he had made while I climbed down the rope. I dropped the last few feet and stepped aside to make room for Mick. The stench was stronger inside the temple, and I gagged. I was surrounded by round pillars that disappeared into the darkness. Like the floor, the pillars were covered with carved scenes of torture, war, human sacrifice and dragon worship.

"Could you bring the light here?" Simon asked. He was standing beside a large mosaic in the floor. We all gathered around Simon to see what he had found. Zhong held out the torch.

In the center of the mosaic was a pyramid. Arching over the pyramid was a dragon with its head and open jaws on the left and its curling tail on the right. Under the dragon's jaws were two men in profile. Both men wore long robes. One had a short beard and shoulder-length hair. He had something in his right hand that he held up to the dragon. The man's left hand held a knife in the chest of the second man. The second man had long hair and a long beard.

"What this shows is obvious," Simon said. "The man with the knife is the prophet. The sacrifice is me."

"Whoever carved this wasted his time," Mick said, "The prophet failed."

"His mistake was in the time and the place. My sacrifice will happen."

"We must continue," Zhong said. Holding the torch, he led us deeper into the temple. We reached an open area with another statue of a large red dragon. It was like the one in the first temple, with its head touching the ceiling and its open jaws hovering over a large stone altar. The top and sides of the altar were stained with ancient black blood.

"We know what happened here," Mick said.

"None of this explains why we're here," Simon replied.

We went deeper into the temple until we reached the back wall. The carved scenes covering and the surrounding pillars were the same as all the others.

"Still nothing to explain why we're here," I said.

"It could be on a side wall," Zhong said. "We will check them next."

"I think I found it," Simon said. He was just outside the edge of the light, running his hand over the back wall.

We stood around him. Zhong held the torch up to the wall. The carved pictures in that part of the wall were different from everything else we had seen. They were arranged in a ten-foot ring that almost touched the ceiling and the floor. Inside the ring was a tall, thin pyramid that reminded me of a spearhead. Four wavy lines extended from the pyramid's base. Just above the peak of the pyramid and in the twelve o'clock position of the ring was a large eye with a vertical slit.

"The eye is the Pathrakotau, the god who sleeps," Simon said. "The pyramid is a third temple.

The lines radiating out from the temple are four rivers. The carvings of the ring are to be interpreted in a clockwise direction, beginning and ending with the eye."

Simon pointed to the first picture after the eye. "A woman has given birth to two sons. The son on her right has the sun around his head. He is her firstborn. A priest holds a knife over the son to her left, which is her second born. He is a sacrifice to the firstborn. The woman is my mother. The prophet is her firstborn. I am the second born."

"And another carving has it all wrong," Mick said.

"It no longer matters." Simon pointed to the next carving. "A man with long hair and a featureless face. He is carrying the second born away from the danger." Simon paused. "I remember now. It was hard to see his face, but I had a strong sense of peace. He was rescuing me! That's how I came to be at the orphanage. He took me there!"

Simon gave the picture a long look before moving on. "In this carving, the priests are offering gifts to the firstborn. They are celebrating his birth. The sun around the firstborn is larger than before. His power as the prophet is growing." He looked at the next image. "This is interesting."

"I don't believe this," Mick said.

The carving showed three men standing to the left of a crouching bull with a surrounding sun. One man was a head taller than the others. Another man held out two objects to the bull like an offering.

"The three men are you," Simon said. "You, Mick, are the tall man. And you, John, are returning the diamonds to the Pathrakotau. The sun around the bull means the awakening of the sleeping god has begun."

"This temple is three thousand years old at least," I said. "How could they know?"

"Actually, this temple is many thousands of years old," Simon said. "As to how they knew, that is a question without an answer."

Simon moved on to the carving at the bottom of the ring. "The sun around the bull is larger. The awakening progresses. The prophet is under the bull. His sun is also larger. This means his power is increasing. He has performed a sacrifice. He lifts a heart up to the bull with his right hand and holds a knife in a man's chest with the left. The pyramid below the prophet has a square temple on its flat peak. We all recognize that.

"We now ascend the ring. In the next carving, the prophet is performing another sacrifice. Below him is another square temple, but unlike the last one, there is no pyramid."

"Is that this temple?" Zhong asked.

"Yes. To the left of the prophet is a coiled dragon. The line between the dragon and the prophet and his sacrifice is a wall."

I had a bad feeling. "What wall is that?"

As soon as I said the words, I heard a scratching sound. We all froze. There was a second scratch, louder than the first.

"It's coming from behind the wall," Mick whispered.

"Simon, we must finish quickly," Zhong said.

"This next carving shows two armies facing each other," Simon said, speaking rapidly. "The army on the left is led by a dragon. The dragon's jaws are spread, ready to devour the enemy. In the next image, the sun arounds the bull and almost fills the image. The awakening of Pathrakotau is almost complete. Next to last is the prophet performing sacrifices in a narrow temple, the same one we see at the center of the ring. The sacrifices in this third temple complete the awakening of the Pathrakotau. That brings us back to the top of the ring and the eye. The eye now represents the awakened god."

A loud boom echoed through the temple. Sand and gravel rained down from the ceiling. Something huge had rammed the other side of the wall, and we weren't waiting to see what. We ran for the temple's entrance.

Zhong and Mick yanked me up through the opening. I rolled to the side to make room for Simon. We heard an intense cawing overhead. The crows filled the sky like a swirling, angry black cloud. We ran down the hill with the dust cloud hovering over the far end of the valley. The dragon men had arrived.

We had to chase down our camels, which had wandered. We mounted them and kicked them to a fast trot up the closest hill to the north and down the other side into the desert.

We had ridden several miles beyond the hills when there was a deafening explosion behind us. A blast of hot air made the camels stumble and almost knocked us from our saddles. Everyone looked back.

A thick column of black smoke boiled up from the location of the temple and engulfed the crows. The smoke changed into a colossal black dragon. It swung it massive head and empty blue eyes in our direction. It watched us briefly before spreading huge bat-like wings, opening its jaws and giving off a thunderous roar. The camels panicked and began moaning and staggering. We whipped their haunches with sticks to keep them running. Omar had given us the sticks for situations exactly like this.

Thousands of dragon men poured over the hills and raced toward us. They looked like ants compared with the dragon. As if taking a cue from the dragon men, the dragon stepped over the hills. It lowered its head and ran after us, its long tail whipping the air. The dragon outran the dragon men and crushed them under his feet.

The dragon was also faster than the camels. The distance between us and it narrowed quickly. I thought the camels were already galloping as fast as they could, but with the dragon closing in on them, they moaned and ran faster than I thought possible. The camels no longer needed the whipping to keep going. We had to hold our saddles with both hands to keep from being thrown off.

I was thinking that things couldn't get worse when I heard barks behind us. I didn't have to look to know what it was, but I couldn't resist glancing back. At least fifty black jackals were charging under and around the dragon in their pursuit of us. They were faster than the dragon and the dragon men and would reach us long before anyone or anything else did.

"A rider!" Mick called out.

I looked forward once again. Six hundred yards ahead, at the top of a sand dune, was a man on a white horse. He had a long gray beard and wore the flowing black robe and head-cloth of the Bedouins, the nomads of the Arabian Desert. Zhong pulled his camel's reins to direct it toward the rider. The other three camels followed instinctively.

We started up the dune with the jackals minutes behind us and howling at the closeness of their prey. The rider motioned for us to follow. He rode down the far side of the dune and out of sight.

The jackals were seconds away when we reached the top and started down the back of the dune. A line of white-robed Bedouins stood on the next dune with their rifles aimed at the top of the dune we were on. Our camels sensed the need to get out of the line of fire and leaped down the back of the dune, carrying us with them.

The Arabs opened fire along the entire line. I felt the wisps of bullets piercing the air above my head. The bangs were followed by yelps and howls from the jackals.

The Arab in black waited calmly at the bottom of the ravine between the two dunes. We yanked hard on our reins to stop our camels beside him.

The Arabs kept up a solid barrage of bullets. The shooting ceased when the yelps stopped. Bleeding jackal bodies covered the top and back of the dune behind us. The Arab in black urged his horse up the second dune and waved for us to follow. His horse climbed easily, while our camels struggled to keep up.

At the top of the dune, the other Arabs had already mounted their horses. There were more than a hundred of them. All the horses were Arabians and decorated with braided manes and tails and weavings of varying colors. The Arabs rode north away from the dragon and the dragon men at a pace our camels could maintain. The Arabs opened a gap leading into their center for the Arab in black, who was obviously their leader, and the four of us. The Arabs closed in behind us.

At our current pace, the dragon would overtake us. I glanced back. The dragon was nowhere to be seen. The dragon men had reversed direction and were running back to the valley. A thin column of smoke rose from the valley in the location of the temple. That explained where the dragon had gone. The prophet had already begun his human sac-rifices. The dragon had returned to the temple to receive his part of the offerings.

Arabs in three groups of ten split off from the main group and galloped hard to the east, west and north. The rest of the riders formed a column of four across behind their leader and us. The leader kept the column heading north at a pace our camels struggled to maintain. As usual, the camels jerked us in all directions. I envied the flowing ride the Arabian horses gave their riders.

We had been riding for twenty minutes when an Arab galloped up from our right and rode next to his leader. The men spoke in low voices without slowing the pace. The Arab nodded and then galloped in the direction from where he had come. The leader shouted, and everyone's pace slowed to a walk.

He looked up and frowned. With perfect English and a British accent, he said, "I do not like those birds."

With so much happening, I hadn't realized the crows were there.

"The birds are spies for the prophet of the dragon men," Simon said.

"Yes, the prophet," the leader replied. "Our enemy has finally arrived." He turned in his saddle to face us. "I am Shareef. I wish to know your names."

Simon bowed his head. "Sir, I am Simon. These are my friends: Zhong, Mick and John."

"Thank you for saving us," I said.

Shareef gave a small nod and faced forward. "Tell me why you are here."

"I ask myself the same thing every day," Mick said.

"How do you answer yourself?"

"I don't have an answer, other than a man stands by his mates, no matter what."

"Mates. Are they like comrades in arms?"

Mick nodded. "Same idea. But ask my mates why we're here. They'll say it's our destiny."

"Ah, destiny," Shareef said. "The answer to all questions. What do you know of the prophet's destiny?"

"His destiny is to awaken the dragon god who sleeps," Simon said.

Shareef nodded. "And now he has succeeded."

"Not yet," Simon replied.

"Then what did I see?"

"The dragon you saw is the prophet's servant, not his god," Simon explained. "His god still sleeps, but its awakening has begun. The complete awakening requires sacrifices in three temples. The prophet has already performed the sacrifices in the temple to the south. The second temple is in the Valley of the Kings, which is why he is here. Even as we speak, he is inside the temple performing the required sacrifices. Once he is finished, he will lead his army to a third temple. After he performs the sacrifices there, the dragon god will awake."

"These sacrifices, I assume they are human," Shareef said.

136

"Yes."

"After this god awakens, what happens next?"

"The dragon god will rule this world, and his prophet will rule with him."

"How do you know these things?"

"Most of this knowledge came at great risk to ourselves," Simon replied. "Mick, John and I were almost sacrifices in the first temple."

"You were fortunate to escape."

"It wasn't luck," I said. "Zhong saved us."

Shareef looked at Zhong. "You are a very capable man."

Zhong bowed slightly. "As are my friends."

Shareef looked forward. "Why does this prophet gather his army? Sacrifices do not require an army."

"The army will force men to worship and obey the prophet and his god," Simon explained. "And kill those who will not kneel before them."

While it made sense, it was not something we knew before. I assumed Simon was speaking from new knowledge.

"Tell me about the third temple," Shareef said.

"We just learned about it," Simon replied. "We saw it in the wall carvings inside the second temple. That's where we were before we rode out of the valley. The third temple is a tower. It has four rivers meeting at its base. That is all we know."

"Where four rivers come together," Shareef said, pulling his beard. "I know of no such a place." He fell silent as he considered what he had heard. We rode quietly and waited for him to speak.

"As a child, I had a dream. I was standing on the peak of a pyramid," he said finally. "Below me was an army filling the desert, as far as I could see. The evil of that army was palpable, and my fear of this evil woke me from the dream. The dream never returned, but the memory has always been with me.

"Eight days ago, I dreamt I was on a dune looking toward the Valley of the Kings. Four men rode out of the valley, pursued by a dark dragon, many thousands of men, and black animals unlike any I had ever seen. I awoke with the strongest sense that the world is on the sharp edge between good and evil, that the slightest touch will topple the world to one side or the other.

"I left immediately with my men. We arrived at the dune of my dream four days ago and waited for you to appear." Shareef turned in his saddle to look in our faces. "I believe your touch will decide the direction the world will fall."

That was a lot to take in. The four of us rode in silence.

Mick was the first to speak. "Sir, can I ask where we're going?"

"The desert of Sinai."

"That's a long ride," I said.

"Three days by horse."

"And by camel?" Mick asked.

"Too long. But that is about to be remedied."

Four Arabs on Arabian horses crested a sand dune ahead of us and halted. Each man held the reins to an Arabian horse without a rider. All the horses had braided manes and tails and weavings like the ones around us.

Shareef halted us in front of the four riders. "Gentlemen, there is no greater joy than riding an Arabian horse through the desert. Please, dismount your camels."

He did not need to tell us twice. As soon our feet hit the sand, the Arabs transferred our water and supply bags to the Arabians. They slapped the haunches of the camels and sent them trotting away.

We mounted the Arabians and, with a light touch of the reins, they stepped into position behind Shareef. Shareef raised his hand, and the column of riders galloped away. Our horses kept up easily. After the camel's jerking motions, riding the Arabian was like flying.

CHAPTER EIGHT

S hareef halted the column at the town of El Suweis on the western shore of the Gulf of Suez. A small patch of white appeared on the far shore. A sail had been unfurled, and a ferry had begun its crossing.

Shareef looked up and frowned. The crows were dark spots circling high above our heads. "We cannot allow the prophet to see any more than he has."

He called out. His men dismounted and pulled the rifles from their saddles. They aimed at the crows and then fired. The crows did not startle or alter their slow circles. The men fired a second time and a third, but the crows did not react. They were too high for the bullets to reach them, and they knew it.

"I did not expect to succeed," Shareef said. "But the attempt was necessary. We will decide our next step after we've completed the crossing."

"Can't you do something?" I whispered to Simon.

He shook his head. "Not yet."

It was forty minutes before the ferry reached our shore. Two men were on the ferry. They dropped the sail and held it in place with long poles. Shareef and the four of us led our horses onto the deck. Shareef nodded, and the men poled us out to the deeper water before resetting the sail. There was room for at least twenty more riders and their horses. I did not understand why Shareef did not fill the ferry. Not doing so meant more trips for the ferry and a slow crossing. But it was not our place to question Shareef, and none of us said a word.

We were fifty yards from shore when Zhong pointed to the Arabs left behind. They mounted their horses, strapped their rifles sideways across their shoulders and urged their horses into the water. The horses waded forward until they had to swim. The riders helped the horses by using their hands to paddle. The Arabs and their horses quickly caught up to the ferry and passed it.

"Impressive," Zhong said.

Shareef smiled. "Only an Arabian can swim this distance. You are all experienced riders, but you are not prepared for this. That is why we use the ferry."

Shareef's men were waiting beside their horses when the ferry touched the far shore. As we led our horses off the ferry, Shareef looked up. "We cannot continue while they watch. We will make camp here and consider our options."

Simon handed his horse's reins to me. "Shareef, may I borrow a bow?"

"A bow? The prophet is still laughing at our last failure."

"Please, Shareef, allow me to try." Simon turned his face to the sky and extended his arms straight out, palms open.

Shareef spoke. A man placed a bow in Simon's left hand and a quiver in his right. Everyone watched to see he would do.

Simon pulled the quiver over his right shoulder. He nocked an arrow and aimed at the crows. The air around him began to shimmer like floating golden dust. The shimmering expanded and coalesced into a transparent golden shell shaped like a muscular man, eighteen feet tall. He had a smooth beardless face and long hair. He wore a loincloth and sandals with interlaced straps that reached to his knees. Like Simon, he had a quiver of arrows over his right shoulder and a nocked arrow.

Simon was visible inside with the golden man surrounding him like body armor. The golden man's quiver, bow and arrow surrounded Simon's. Then, moving as one, the golden man and Simon pulled back their bowstrings and released.

THUMP.

The golden man/Simon's arrow soared into the sky. A crow burst into a small cloud of black feathers. The two other crows fluttered higher in surprise.

The golden man/Simon quickly notched and released a second arrow and then a third. Each arrow hit a crow with another burst of black. The bodies of all three crows tumbled down and landed on the sand before us.

The golden man/Simon lowered their bow. The golden man shimmered and faded away until all that remained was Simon. He returned the bow and quiver to the man who had lent them to him. Then he stepped to where he could see us all and bowed. Our stunned silence was replaced by cheers and shouts. Then Shareef's men began chanting words over and over:

"Aldahahab almahareeb! Aldahahab almahareeb! Aldahahab almahareeb!"

"What are they saying?" Zhong asked.

"Golden Warrior," Shareef said. "That is the name they have given to what Simon became."

The sun was touching the western horizon as we galloped toward a wall of sand. The wall extended as far as I could see to the north and south.

"Our first defensive line," Shareef said, slowing our pace to a walk.

We rode up one side of the wall and down the other into a trench that ran the length of the wall. Men and women behind the wall and in the trench came to attention. They wore the clothing and uniforms of different nations. They saluted or bowed to

Shareef with their eyes on the four of us, but mainly Simon. Then they began chanting the same words over and over in several languages.

"*Gouden Streejer! Gouden Streejer! Gouden Streejer!*"

"*Gariay deeor! Gariay deeor! Gariay deeor!*"

"*Gayrrayro del oro! Gayrrayro del oro! Gayrrayro del oro!*"

"*GoldenKreeger! GoldenKreeger! GoldenKreeger!*"

"I assume they're chanting 'Golden Warrior,'" I said.

Shareef nodded. "I do not know most of the languages, but I am certain you are correct."

"How do they know?" Mick asked. "We just got here."

"We have patrols and scouts everywhere," Shareef said, "and nothing travels as fast as good news."

When we were beyond the defensive line, Shareef sped the column up to a trot. "Our main line of defense is ten miles ahead," he said. "Are you aware the prophet has a second and far larger army?"

"We were told by the man who gave us our camels," Zhong replied.

"That is the army of your dream, is it not?" Simon asked.

Shareef nodded. "Yes. The first dragon men began gathering around the Giza pyramids three months ago. I have not seen it for myself, but our scouts estimate their numbers now to be at least four hundred thousand strong. The prophet's army grows larger every day."

"Sir, how large is your army?" Zhong asked.

"Less than half the size of the Giza army. We are doing what we can to prepare. We show the enemy only what makes us appear weaker than we are. We want the prophet to be overconfident, prone to mistakes. That was why I could not let the crows see us."

"Deception is an important weapon of war," Zhong said.

"That is true," Shareef replied, "but a hidden weakness is still a weakness."

"If you are so badly outnumbered," Mick said, "why do the soldiers stay?"

"For the same reasons you came. Some believe it is their destiny to be here. Others sense our stand against the prophet and his army is crucial to the survival of the world, as we know it. Many are like you, Mick. They came and stay for their comrades in arms.

"Ironically, until I spoke with you, no one in our army, myself included, knew what we hoped to accomplish by stopping the prophet. After speaking with you, I now know our purpose has something to do with the third temple."

As we passed through the second and main defensive line, the soldiers guarding the wall came to attention and stared at us, but mainly at Simon. The man who had become the Golden Warrior was easy to recognize with his long white hair, white beard, and black skin. The soldiers chanted words that I knew meant "Golden Warrior."

Shareef gave an order, and his Arab escort rode north. He kept the four of us riding in the same direction. He led us up a hill and then halted us at the top. "This is our army."

Before us was a flat plain and the main camp. The fire pits surrounded by soldiers were like we had seen at Djibouti, and close to the same number. To the right were scattered glints of reflected light and the clangs of metal on metal as thousands of soldiers practiced with swords and knives. There was no gunfire. Cannons waited silently in long straight rows to our left. For an army training for war, there was a disturbing lack of noise.

"Why do the men not train with the guns and cannons?" Zhong asked.

"There is not enough ammunition or gunpowder for training," Shareef said. "We must conserve what we have for the fighting. Come." He led us down the hill into the camp.

As we rode through the camp, soldiers ran to us from everywhere. They massed around us, saluting and bowing, shouting and smiling, chanting and pointing at Simon. The press of the soldiers slowed us to a crawl. Shareef smiled and nodded and did nothing to prohibit the men and women from enjoying the moment.

It soon became obvious that our destination was a large canvas tent on the far edge of the camp. The tent was a tenth the size of the prophet's tent. When we reached the tent, guards took our horses' reins. Two guards held back the tent flaps, and we followed Shareef inside. The floor was covered with rugs and large pillows. Jugs of water and baskets of dates waited in the center. Two soldiers stood at attention.

Shareef gestured for us to sit. "First, we refresh ourselves. Then we meet with the commanders."

Shareef had just handed the water bag to Zhong when the tent flaps were pulled aside. Forty soldiers funneled through the opening. They appeared to be officers with their second-in-commands. They formed a circle around the inside of the tent with us in the center. They quietly studied our faces, but mainly Simon's.

"It appears our meeting with the commanders has begun," Shareef said and stood. We followed suit.

"Gentlemen," Shareef said to the soldiers, "I wish to introduce Zhong, Mick, John and Simon."

We bowed as Shareef said our names. He went around the tent and introduced the commanders. The only name that stuck with me was Tong Rhongi. He was a short Mongolian shaped like a barrel. He was the only man I'd ever seen who had a face as ferocious as Rasheed, the Thug leader who had chased us across India.

"These are the men?" a British commander asked.

Shareef nodded. "These are the men."

"The reports are hard to believe," an Indian commander said. "And you saw all this yourself?"

"Yes, I saw it all, and so did my men," Shareef replied. "Everything is exactly as you were told. The jackals and the dragon. I would like everyone to sit."

The commanders sat and listened intently as Shareef described the events at the Valley of the Kings. He repeated what we had told him about our escape from the first temple. When he described Simon becoming the Golden Warrior and killing the crows, everyone except Tong Rhongi kept their eyes on Simon. Tong Rhongi remained motionless with his face stern and his eyes fixed on the center of the circle.

When Shareef finished, Tong Rhongi spoke. "My commander, I apologize. I was wrong to doubt you and your dream. But these men and their Golden Warrior who kills birds, they change nothing. They offer nothing that would alter our battle plans."

"The Golden Warrior has already made a difference," Shareef said. "He has given our soldiers, and some of you in this tent, what we needed most desperately. Hope."

"And once the battle begins," Tong Rhongi said, "this hope he has generated will disappear like morning mist under the desert sun."

"Sir, may I speak?" Simon asked.

Shareef nodded. "Please proceed."

"I do not want there to be misunderstandings about me and what I did. Tong Rhongi is correct. You cannot put your hope in the Golden Warrior, because he will never return."

"Why not?" Shareef asked.

"I am a magician, and the Golden Warrior came from my magic. But my magic is not like other magicians. It never repeats itself. The Golden Warrior cannot happen twice."

"So, you are a magician," Tong Rhongi said and looked around the tent. "My comrades, the Golden Warrior was nothing but an illusion!"

"He was no illusion," Mick said. "He was real."

"Zhong and I saw it," I added.

"As did I and my men," Shareef said.

"The other thing you should know," Simon continued, "is I am destined to die, and my time is near. I am to be a sacrifice to a dragon."

"The dragon that was chasing you?" a Dutch commander asked.

"I do not know."

"You're refusing to help us?" a Russian commander asked.

"No. I want you to understand the Golden Warrior will not be there to help you, but I will. Until my destiny takes me, I offer you as much as any man can offer. I will fight and die with you."

Tong Rhongi turned to Shareef. "My commander, did I not warn you? We cannot trust in dreams or invisible powers! We live or die by our own hands!"

The tent became dead quiet. The hope offered by the Golden Warrior was gone, replaced by palpable despair in every heart except Tong Rhongi's. The army and its commanders were so desperate for help they had grasped onto the Golden Warrior as the answer to their prayers.

A man rushed into the tent and spoke into Shareef's ear.

"Gentlemen!" Shareef shouted, and the room went silent. "The prophet's southern army has been sighted. We must go to the command tent for a briefing. No one is to discuss the Golden Warrior outside this tent. Let the soldiers enjoy their hope while it lasts." He looked at the four of us. "A soldier will escort you to my tent. Please remain there until I send for you."

We followed Shareef through the tent flaps. I was surprised to find a sea of soldiers waiting outside. They cheered as soon as we appeared. The soldiers who had followed us to the tent had never left. Thousands more had joined them while we were inside.

Shareef smiled with a confidence I knew he did not feel. "You will stay with me," he said to us. "Say nothing."

The commanders surrounded us and guided us through the soldiers. We were jostled on all sides by shouting, excited women and men. Everyone wanted to see the men who would help them defeat the dragon army. Unable to ignore them, Zhong, Mick, Simon and I acknowledged the soldiers with nods.

Mick and I felt like frauds.

We followed Shareef through a perimeter of armed guards into a second tent. The floor inside was covered with woven rugs with intricate patterns. A lieutenant and five soldiers stood around a large table in the center. On the table was a large map with hundreds of colored pieces. The soldiers were moving the pieces when we entered. They stepped back immediately and came to attention, their eyes focused on Simon.

We stood behind Shareef as he and the commanders took their positions around the table. Zhong, Mick, Simon and I looked over shoulders. The map was of Egypt and the Sinai Peninsula. Two lines of red markers paralleled the eastern shore of the Gulf of Suez and ran north to south. They were the defensive positions of Shareef's army. Based on the scale of the map, the two lines were four miles long and one and ten miles from the gulf. A cluster of red markers behind the second line was the main camp and our current location.

Sixty miles to the west of the Gulf of Suez, at Giza, was a large cluster of blue markers. It had more than twice the number of the red markers. That was the prophet's army gathering at the pyramids. Thirty miles to the south of Giza was a second group of blue markers larger than the number of the red army. It was the prophet's southern army. At the northern edge of the southern army was a single black marker.

"Ravi, you may begin," Shareef said.

The lieutenant nodded to his men, and they quickly left the tent. He pointed at the blue markers with a long thin stick. "These are the current positions and strengths of the prophet's two armies. We expect the southern army to join with the northern army in three days. Once the armies come together, we estimate they will need seven days to organize themselves before beginning their march east. I estimate another week before they reach the Suez and begin their crossing. That gives us two and a half weeks to finish our preparations."

"What is the black piece?" a British commander asked.

"That is the prophet's dragon. It leads the southern army. The prophet is in the center of this army."

Ravi pointed to the northern tip of the Gulf of Suez. "We expect the enemy to cross here, where the water is shallow. The crossing will force the prophet's army into a narrow column. When they reach our side of the gulf, we expect them to spread out their frontline before advancing."

"And how wide will that be?" Tong Rhongi asked.

"At least six miles," Ravi said.

"After they finish expanding their line, what will be the depth of their soldiers?" a French commander asked.

"With the addition of the southern army, we estimate they will be thirty men deep, twice our previous estimate." Ravi pointed to the red markers. "Our lines of defense are four miles wide. We must extend them at least one additional mile on both ends. If we don't, the dragon army will simply march around our flanks."

"If we extend our lines, how does that change the depth of our troops?" Tong Rhongi asked.

"Our soldiers spread over a six-mile line." Ravi paused and studied the map. "That will give us a depth of five men."

Tong Rhongi sniffed. "You are being overly generous."

"Our five to their thirty." Shareef shook his head. Any other needed changes?"

"We've had to revise our assessments of their cannons. They now have over three thousand. Most of them are larger than ours, and that means greater range. Once they establish their cannons on our side of the gulf, their cannons and ours will be within range of each other. But if we are forced to retreat, the dragon army will be able to keep us within the range of their cannons while staying outside the range of ours. Once that happens, they can pound our lines to dust, and we will be unable to respond."

"Then we must hold our first line of defense," a German commander said.

"Unfortunately, with their troop numbers and ours," Ravi said, "Once the conflict begins, a breach of our first defenses is just a matter of time. When it happens…." He shook his head.

"Is nothing superior about our army?" Shareef asked.

Ravi looked at him. "I am sorry, sir, but no. Our army continues to grow. More men, women, weapons and supplies arrive each day. But the dragon army is also growing, and much quicker than ours. The arrival of the army from the south has made everything even more difficult."

Tong Rhongi grunted. "Men have always been drawn to evil over good. But such men will not sacrifice themselves for another. We must hit them hard when they come ashore. Attack before they are ready! Threaten their lives, and they will scatter. I promise you that!"

"We know and respect your thoughts, my friend," Shareef said, but we have already decided. With the enemy's vastly superior numbers, our only option is a defensive war. Ravi, thank you. I think we have heard enough."

"Sir," Ravi said, "I must remind the commanders that our plans assume that the prophet's army will march directly east following their crossing. If they advance in a different direction, our lines could be off by as much as three miles. Flanking us would be easy. The piece we lack for planning our defenses is the prophet's purpose. If we knew that, we might be able to determine his destination. We could then better position our army for maximum effect."

"Simon," Shareef said. "This would be a good time to tell us what you and your comrades know about the prophet and the third temple."

"I'd like to point out," Mick said, "everything he tells you, we learned the hard way."

"That is true," Shareef said, "As we rode here, I was told Simon, Mick and John were almost sacrifices at the first temple."

"Zhong saved us," I said.

"Saving us is his specialty," Mick added.

"Gentlemen," Simon said, "the prophet's sole purpose is to awaken his god. To accomplish that, he must perform blood sacrifices in three temples. He has performed sacrifices in the first and second temples. His purpose now is to reach the third temple and perform the final sacrifices. Once that is done, his god will awaken."

"How do you know this?" Tong Rhongi asked.

"We found the second temple in the Valley of the Kings," Simon said. "A wall of carvings inside shows the prophet performing sacrifices in the third temple and the awakening of the god. Once his army crosses the water, the prophet will want to reach the temple as soon as possible. He will lead them straight to the third temple."

"You speak like you know this prophet," an African commander said.

"He is my twin brother," Simon replied.

Surprised murmuring rippled throughout the tent.

"If you are his brother," an Italian commander said, "how do we know you're not misleading us to help him defeat us?"

"You can't know, at least not for certain. But events are coming that will prove my friends and I can be trusted."

"So, where is this third temple?" Tong Rhongi asked. "Without the location, your information is useless."

"That we don't know," Simon admitted. "But a carving inside the second temple contains a significant clue. The temple has four rivers coming out from its base. Find a place where four rivers meet, and you will have the location."

Shareef looked around the circle. "Does anyone know of such a place?"

The commanders shrugged and shook their heads.

"Sir," Zhong said, "may I have a map that shows Africa and all of Arabia?"

Shareef nodded to Ravi, who opened a long metal box, pulled out a map and unrolled it on the table next to the other map. Zhong picked up two red markers and placed one on the volcano at Djibouti and the other on the temple in the valley.

"May I draw on the map?" Zhong asked.

"The map is yours," Ravi replied.

We watched as Zhong took a straight edge and a pencil and drew a line between the two markers. He drew a second line perpendicular to the first. It began in the middle of the first line and ran east across Arabia. Zhong placed an X on the eastern Arabia part of the second line. He drew two more lines, one from each temple to the X. The last two lines with the first one for a base made a long, narrow triangle.

"What is this, Zhong?" Tong Rhongi asked for all of us.

"In ancient cultures, the placement of temples was never random. They always had special meaning," Zhong said. "The third temple is a narrow triangle, I assumed a line between the first two temples would be the base of the triangle. I drew the last two lines to form a triangle with the same shape as the temple in the carving." Zhong placed a third red marker on the tip of the triangle. "This is the location of the third temple and the meeting point of the four rivers."

Everyone crowded closer to the map. The marker was just south of Baghdad.

"I have been through that area many times," Ravi said. "There are two rivers in that location—the Tigris and the Euphrates—not four."

"That is true now," a Jewish commander said. "But our earliest writings speak of four rivers at that site. That is also the location of the ancient city of Ur and the Tower of Babel."

"All right. Let us assume the third temple is there," Ravi said. He picked up the straight edge and the pencil and drew a line from the tip of the triangle to the point where the dragon army would cross the gulf. The line passed through the northern ends of our first and second defensive lines. "If what Simon said about the prophet's army heading straight for this temple is true, our army is in the wrong position, and he will flank us immediately."

The commanders launched into a loud debate over the validity of what they had heard and seen and what to do if it was true.

"Silence!" Tong Rhongi shouted. The excited voices died down slowly.

Once the commanders were quiet, Tong Rhongi continued. "I admit this is all very intriguing, and for those of you who pray, it feels like an answer to your prayers. But it is my duty to remind everyone here that what we've heard comes from a man we have known less than an hour. We cannot not act on any of this, not until all this is confirmed by other sources."

Shareef sighed and nodded. "As always, Tong Rhongi, your wisdom protects us from making serious mistakes. We cannot act on this information until it is confirmed."

"And how, sir, do we confirm it?" an Irish commander asked.

Shareef thought for a moment and then shrugged. "I do not know."

Shareef and the commanders had the four of us ride with them as they inspected their defenses. We reached the northern end of the first defensive line and dismounted at the top of a hill. The commanders looked to the north and the west. No one said anything, but they were studying the ground and thinking about the preparations we would need if Simon and Zhong's information proved accurate. The soldiers manning the defensive line watched us closely, sensing the confusion and wondering what it was about.

"Gentlemen!" the African commander shouted. "To the west!"

High in the sky over the Gulf of Suez was a small black cloud. It grew larger as we watched. The crows were back, hundreds of them.

Tong Rhongi glared at the birds, opening and closing his fists in frustration. "They will soon see our defenses and our weaknesses! Is there nothing we can do to stop them?"

Simon dismounted and walked past Shareef to the front of the hill, his eyes fixed on the crows. He stuck out both arms, palms up. Tong Rhongi leapt down from his saddle. He grabbed the bow and quiver from his saddle and placed them in Simon's hands. Then he quickly stepped back to see what would happen next.

Simon nocked an arrow and aimed at the crows. The air around him began to shimmer like gold and formed a nearly transparent golden shell, with him in the center. The shell had the shape of a huge, heavily muscled warrior. It wasn't supposed to happen, but it did. The Golden Warrior had returned.

The Golden Warrior/Simon pulled back their bowstrings and released them as one. Their arrow shot into the sky and quickly disappeared. The Golden Warrior/Simon continued nocking and releasing arrows with machine-like speed and precision. They moved so fast that their arms and hands were difficult to see. One black dot dropped from the cloud, then another and another. Once the crows began falling from the sky, it did not stop.

Shareef, Tong Rhongi, the other commanders and the soldiers guarding the defensive line cheered wildly. Mick and I shouted our excitement along with them. Zhong nodded his head in prayer.

The black cloud of crows turned back, leaving a trail of falling birds. It soon became a barely visible speck. The Golden Warrior/Simon continued releasing arrows long after the cloud passed from view.

Finally, the Golden Warrior/Simon lowered his bow. The gold shimmered and dissolved until all that remained was Simon. Simon handed the bow and arrows back to Thong Rhongi, who smiled and gave him a bone-crushing hug. Shareef and the commanders massed around Simon, grabbing his shoulders and pounding his back.

Zhong, Mick and I worked our way through the crowd. Mick and I hugged Simon, while Zhong held his shoulder.

"Now that's what I call magic!" Mick shouted.

"Couldn't happen at a better time!" I yelled.

Simon smiled. "That was a total surprise!"

News of the Golden Warrior's return spread through the army like wildfire. Shouting and cheering soldiers swarmed us as we rode into camp and brought us to a halt. We dismounted, and a company of soldiers, led by Ravi, forced a way through the crowd to the command tent.

When we finally pushed through the tent flaps, Tong Rhongi grabbed Simon by the shoulders. "You said the magic never repeats!"

"Until now, that was true."

Tong Rhongi looked around at all the faces. "Today you and I have both learned that it is sometimes good to be wrong!" Everyone laughed. "Please tell the Golden Warrior, he is welcome to come back anytime!"

We cheered and laughed.

Shareef raised his hand for quiet. "My friends, can I assume we now have the confirmation we need to believe that what these four men said is true?"

All the commanders, including Tong Rhongi, roared their approval.

Before dawn broke the next day, the army had already begun lengthening and shifting our defensive lines to the north. When the four of us weren't helping the commanders, we were digging alongside the soldiers.

On the third day, Shareef had us join the commanders on a ride to evaluate our progress in changing the defensive lines. As we rode past the soldiers, they briefly stopped to bow and salute before returning to the work.

When we reached the new northern end of our first defensive line, Shareef halted at the top of a dune with clear visibility of the line and soldiers.

"Your assessment, gentlemen," Shareef said. "Will we complete the fortifications before the attack?"

Tong Rhongi shook his head. "My commander, the answer is obvious. We will not complete the changes in time. That said, I prefer incomplete fortifications in the correct location to the best defenses where they are useless. We can only do our best with the time we have."

"Sir," Zhong said, "May I ride the line of the enemy's approach?"

"To what purpose?" Shareef asked. "There is nothing but sand between us and the gulf."

"I understand, sir, but I would still like to examine the ground."

Shareef nodded. "Very well."

The commanders resumed their discussion as Zhong rode down the face of the dune toward the water. Mick, Simon and I watched him ride at a walking pace, his eyes on the ground. Zhong never did anything without an excellent reason. As he slowly disappeared, I wondered what the reason was.

We entered the command tent and assembled around the map table. The commanders immediately began a loud debate about the inadequacy of our defenses and what to do about it. Suddenly, Zhong was standing beside Mick, Simon and me. He did not speak, only listened intently.

Shareef raised a hand, and the discussion ceased. "Gentlemen, the debate on how to strengthen our defenses is over. We must decide what to do with the limited time we have remaining. Your recommendations, please."

"Sir, I am not a commander," Zhong said, "but, with your permission, I wish to make several proposals."

"Zhong, I do not say this out of disrespect," Shareef replied, "but we do not have the time to consider any other ideas."

"My first proposal will provide the time we need to complete all preparations," Zhong said. "It is based on the teachings of Sun Tzu."

"Who is Sun Tzu?" a Greek commander asked.

"A soldier who has not heard of Sun Tzu?" Tong Rhongi said. "He is the Chinese master of war! My commander, I suggest we hear Zhong out."

"Very well," Shareef said, "but please, Zhong. Be brief."

"Sun Tzu taught to attack when the enemy does not expect attack," Zhong said. "Attack where he is weak and unprepared. Attack with fire. Attack like a thunderbolt. I propose using these teachings to attack the dragon army's camp. A successful attack will give us the time to complete the changes to our defenses and my other proposals."

"Attack the dragon army in their camp?" Tong Rhongi said. "My apologies, commander. I did not think Zhong would waste our time with the impossible."

"My proposal will succeed," Zhong insisted. "I will prove it to Shareef and Tong Rhongi, but after they vow not to discuss what they see and hear with the rest of you. To allow anyone else to see the proof would violate my vows. The rest of the commanders must agree to allow Shareef and Tong Rhongi to decide for all of them."

"Why should I decide?" Tong Rhongi asked.

"Because you are the most difficult to convince," Zhong said. His response was met by scattered chuckles.

"No more discussion," Shareef said, looking around the room. "Vote to agree or not agree to Zhong's conditions. Your vote must be unanimous.

Tong Rhongi and I will not vote. Your vote, gentlemen."

All the commanders said, "I agree," or nodded their agreement.

"Very well," Shareef said. "Will everyone, please wait outside?"

Simon, Mick and I stood to leave, but Zhong put his hand on my arm.

"I need you three to remain," Zhong said. "Especially you, Simon."

"Ah," Tong Rhongi said. "The proposal uses the Golden Warrior!"

"No," Zhong replied, but it does require Simon, the magician."

The night was pitch black and moonless. Zhong, Tong Rhongi and I were on top of a sand dune. The only lights above us were the stars. Below us was an endless carpet of flickering lights stretching in every direction—the dragon army's campfires. The prophet's large tent glowed at the center. The pyramids of Giza created large black voids beyond the campfires to our right.

Ironically, our plan when we boarded the cruiser in Bombay had been to visit the pyramids. We had finally succeeded in reaching them, but we could not see them.

The attack on the dragon army camp would begin in three minutes. Even in the darkness, I felt

Tong Rhongi's growing excitement. The rest of our ten-man team waited on dunes to both sides of us. Simon, Mick and their ten-man team waited on the far side of the dragon army.

Shareef and Tong Rhongi had initially rejected Zhong's proposal. But after he and Simon demonstrated their abilities to make Mick and me invisible, they quickly agreed.

Zhong's proposal required Simon's knowledge of explosive powders. Simon supervised 250 men in the making of the bombs and the grenades carried by each team member. The bombs were large cloth bags filled with his explosive powder and timed fuses. The grenades were small bags bulging with the powder and containing pieces of iron and flint tied together. When the grenade hit, the steel and the flint would strike each other and create a spark to ignite the powder

Our two teams had used Zhong and Simon's ability to create invisibility to sneak in and out of the dragon army's camp. We had planted bombs at the ammunition and powder stores, the armories, the prophet's tent and along the lines of cannons.

Suddenly, we saw bursts of light from the large central tent, followed by ear-pounding explosions. The attack had begun.

Dragon men everywhere jumped to their feet and shouted. A second series of flashes and explosions ripped through the munitions storage, setting off more booms and flashes as the ammunition and gunpowder stores exploded, followed by screams and shouts. Next came scattered explosions throughout the camp, with more screaming and shouting.

Our team leapt to its feet, and each of us threw five grenades into the dragon men's camp. Then we ran down the back of the dunes to the next set of dunes, seventy yards away. When we reached the top, we threw more grenades and ran to the next set of dunes. We repeated the pattern until our grenade bags were empty. Zhong now led us at a run back to our horses, which were tethered five hundred yards from the dragon camp.

Suddenly, large groups of dragon men burst from the darkness on both sides of us. Zhong signaled with his hand for us to drop flat. The group on our right ran past us and charged the other dragon men with knives, swords and guns. We heard bangs and screams as the dragon men killed each other.

With the dragon men consumed with killing each other, we continued forward in a crouch. We were almost to the horses when Zhong signaled again for us to drop. I could barely make out the shadows of our restless horses. I counted the shadows of at least eight men standing around them. They were dragon men, because we had left only two soldiers to guard the horses.

Tong Rhongi's shadow gestured for Zhong and me to remain and for the soldiers to follow him. They slipped into the darkness. Two minutes later, the blackness moved on both sides of the dragon men. They grunted and struggled briefly before falling with dull thumps.

Zhong and I leapt up and ran to the horses. Tong Rhongi's short, thick shadow was wiping his knife on a dragon man's pants.

"Bombs have no honor," he whispered. "This is how a warrior kills!"

Our two teams met at the waiting ferry and crossed the gulf together. We had brought our two dead comrades with us, their bodies tied to their horses. It was painful to lose fellow soldiers, but that did not dampen our excitement at the attack's success.

The sun was just above the horizon when we rode across our first defensive line. The soldiers massed around us, forcing us to stop and shouting for a report. Tong Rhongi dismounted and led both teams to the top of a dune, so the soldiers could see and hear us. Tong Rhongi waved his hands for quiet. When he could be heard, he raised his fists into the air and shouted a single word. "Victory!"

The soldiers responded with a roar. Tong Rhongi let them enjoy the victory for several minutes before waving for silence.

"Everything went according to plan," Tong Rhongi said. "It was glorious! Our enemy is still licking his wounds!"

That brought an outburst of laughter. When it quieted down, Tong Rhongi began an account of the attack that was both lively and packed with exaggeration.

We had to stop four more times for massing soldiers, and Tong Rhongi had to describe the attack each time before we finally pushed through the flaps of the command tent. Shareef and the commanders were waiting inside. They welcomed Zhong, Simon, Mick and me with cheers, back slapping and crushing hugs. Then Tong Rhongi gave a report on the attack to the commanders. It was even more embellished than his previous accounts and was constantly interrupted by shouts, questions and laughter.

It took over two hours before Tong Rhongi finished his report. "Now we have the time we need to complete our defenses," he concluded.

The commanders responded with a thundering cheer.

We assembled around the map table. The red markers had been moved to reflect the recent changes to our defensive positions. Many of the changes were the result of Zhong's other proposals.

"You have made significant progress," Zhong observed.

"Men with hope and a clear purpose work hard," Ravi replied. "The latest reports from our scouts indicate the dragon army is in chaos. As Rhongi said, the attack has given us time to finish our preparations."

"Any word about the prophet?" I asked.

"His tent was destroyed," Ravi said, "but the prophet is still among the living. Our scouts heard him haranguing his army for allowing the attack."

"That's disappointing," Mick said.

I agreed with Mick. If anyone deserved to die, it was the prophet.

CHAPTER NINE

T he world was strangely still. It was like Creation was holding its breath. The deep red to the east meant dawn was near, and the dragon army's attack was minutes away.

Mick, Simon and I were dug into the top of our first defensive line. Our weapons were ready beside us. We had spent a long sleepless night at our posts staring into darkness and listening for a sound that was not the lapping of water. Zhong was with the soldiers waiting to unleash the thunderbolts of Sun Tzu.

Our first defensive line had been moved north and one mile from the water's edge. Without the crows to warn him, the prophet believed our first defensive line was still positioned farther south and three miles from the gulf. When we attacked, the element of surprise would be complete.

I felt a touch on my shoulder from Mick. I stared harder into the darkness. At first, I saw nothing. Then part of the blackness moved silently. The dragon army's scouts had arrived. Shadows flowed in from both sides, engulfed the scouts and then pulled back into the darkness. The dragon scouts were gone.

Twenty minutes later, I heard soft sloshing and saw a black mass flowing toward us. I put my rifle butt against my shoulder and positioned my finger beside the trigger. The sloshing became splashing and then crunching as the black mass of dragon men marched across the sand. I placed my finger on the trigger.

When the dragon men were a hundred yards away, the growing light to the east cast a red edge to their shadows. When they were fifty yards away, I expected the signal to open fire, but it didn't come. Then they were forty yards away. Still no signal. There had to be a mix-up. I was about to pull the trigger when a flaming arrow shot into the sky. Our frontline exploded with the bangs and pops of gunfire and the booms of cannons. We fired into the black mass as fast as we could reload. Shouts and screams from the dragon men were everywhere. The first thunderbolt of Sun Tzu had struck!

The dragon army was caught completely off guard. It was many minutes before the sputtering of their return fire became a steady barrage. Enemy bullets thudded into the sand around us and whistled over our heads.

I heard booms from the far side of the gulf as the dragon cannons joined the battle. Cannonballs splashed in the water and hit the beach with jarring explosions. Some of the cannonballs did not explode but bounced across the sand, killing and maiming their own men. A few of the bouncing cannonballs slammed into our defenses, where they embedded themselves harmlessly or exploded, sending showers of sand on our heads.

The dragon men were being slaughtered, but we could not kill them fast enough. Using their overwhelming numbers, they kept coming, their front line edging steadily toward us.

The dragon men were twenty yards away when flaming arrows shot into the sky along our entire line. The arrows arched over and landed among the dragon men a thousand yards away. Everywhere the arrows hit, fires with billowing black smoke flared up. The fires raced north and south, paralleling our defenses and devouring dragon soldiers. Then the flames raced together into an impassable wall of fire and smoke that was fifty yards wide. The wall extended two miles beyond our defenses at both ends.

It was Greek fire, a weapon that had not been used in battle for 1,500 years. The rest of the world had lost the secret of making Greek fire, but Zhong's people still had it. Zhong had supervised three thousand soldiers in creating the tarry mixture and soaking it into the sand in front of our defenses.

The wall of Greek fire split the dragon army. The army on our side of the wall was a size we could defeat. Bugles sounded. Our cavalry charged into the enemy from both flanks. The dragon men in front of us panicked and, unable to retreat, swarmed over the bodies of their dead, straight into our defenses. Vicious hand-to-hand combat broke out everywhere. I stabbed and shot every dragon man I could see. Zhong was suddenly fighting beside me, his arms and legs a blur.

I did not know how long we had been fighting. I pulled my knife from a dragon man and, staggering from exhaustion, looked for the next enemy soldier. But the only soldiers left standing were ours. Dead and injured soldiers covered the sand between our defenses and the wall of fire. The majority of the casualties were dragon men, but many, too many, were our soldiers.

Those of us with minor wounds searched for our severely injured. We had just finished binding their wounds as best we could when the bugles sounded the retreat. The injured who could walk began the nine-mile trek to our second defensive line. The severely injured and those unable to walk were carried to waiting wagons. That left the soldiers who could walk with help. We lifted them onto their feet and half-carried them by holding their arms across our shoulders. The retreat was covered by the Greek fire behind us and the cavalry on our flanks.

We had to leave our dead where they lay. We hated doing it, but we did not have enough time or wagons to bring them.

Simon, Zhong, Mick and I were together. We were each half-carrying a soldier when a soldier rode up, leading four horses without riders. "Sirs, I have been ordered to escort you to the command tent."

"Thank you," Simon said and took the reins for the four horses from the soldier's hand. "Tell the commanders we will come once these soldiers are safe."

The walking wounded and soldiers helping other soldiers stopped to watch as Simon helped his soldier swing onto the saddle of a horse. Following his lead, Zhong, Mick and I lifted our soldiers onto the other horses.

The soldier who had brought the horses smiled. "Very well, sir." He galloped off.

We resumed the long hike, leading the horses by their reins. The men around us walked with new energy.

"My destiny is near," Simon said.

"How near?" Mick asked.

"I die during the next battle.

I looked at him. "What about us?"

"You are not there. I die alone."

"Then you're finally wrong about something," Mick said. "Because we're not leaving you. We're mates now."

"I know you mean what you say, Mick. But you will leave me."

It was late afternoon when we reached the second defensive line. Soldiers took the horses' reins and led them and their wounded riders to the field hospital. We continued to the command tent with soldiers massed around us, shouting and cheering. The guards smiled as they pulled back the tent flaps, and we passed inside.

The commanders leapt to their feet around the map table. They applauded and cheered. Tong Rhongi waved us into the space between Shareef and himself.

"You again inspire the army," Shareef said. "Your march with the wounded meant almost as much as the victory. We all thank you." He looked around the tent. "Gentlemen, our comrades are tired. I suggest we sit."

We were grateful to be off our feet. We gulped the water and devoured the food set before us.

"We have been discussing the battle," Ravi said. "We have succeeded beyond all expectations. Based on initial scouting reports, we estimate the enemy's losses at more than one hundred fifty thousand men."

"A mere dent in their side," Tong Rhongi said. "Do not forget the size of their army."

"What is the number of our losses?" the Spanish commander asked.

Ravi hesitated. "The current estimate is twenty-five thousand."

"A tenth of our army," Tong Rhongi said. "Nine more victories like this, and we will be annihilated!"

The joy of victory disappeared. The tent was filled with a tense silence as everyone absorbed the hard truth.

It was early morning on the third day after the battle. The dark shapes of my mates and the soldiers were barely visible in the growing light. It had been another long sleepless night on our defensive line, staring into darkness.

"It begins," Zhong whispered.

Booms and flashes of light peppered the blackness, followed by distant screams. The dragon army had entered the minefield, another of Zhong's proposals. The mines had been made with Simon's explosive powder. They were like the grenades but much larger. The mines had been buried in the sand at two levels. Those closest to the surface could be detonated with the weight of a man. The deeper mines would only explode when something heavier passed over them, like a wagon or a cannon.

The explosions happened closer and closer as the dragon army marched across their dead and injured. It was many long minutes before the explosions tapered off. The meant the dragon army was beyond the minefield. I heard the quick crunching of their feet.

The early morning light was enough to make out movement five hundred yards away. The dragon army could see us, too, because they gave a thunderous shout and charged. Then the front of their line dropped out of view with shouts of surprise. The soldiers behind them kept coming, but they also dropped out of sight as they pushed blindly forward.

The dragon men were falling into a large trench, another of Zhong's proposals. Our soldiers had dug it twenty feet deep and thirty feet wide. The trench had been camouflaged with a cover of woven sticks and grasses and a layer of sand. It ran parallel to our defensive line and extended three miles beyond the northern and southern ends.

The trench quickly filled with dragon men. Soon they were climbing over each other and out of the trench on our side. They gathered on the sand before us. When they had sufficient numbers, they roared "*Kun tahee!*" and charged. Like before, we held our fire and waited for the signal.

When the dragon men were fifty yards away, a flaming arrow shot into the sky. Rifle and cannon fire broke out along our entire line. We fired as fast as we could reload, killing the dragon men by the tens of thousands. The sand between us and the trench filled with their dead and injured. Soon, the bodies became piles, and the dragon men used the bodies as cover for their advance.

Like before, we couldn't kill them fast enough. The front of the dragon army edged closer. Eventually, they reached our defenses and leaped into our positions. The battle became hand-to-hand, with dragon men everywhere. I fired or stabbed at one dragon man, only to have another attack.

Out of the corner of my eye, I saw a dragon soldier lift a sword to stab me. I was too squeezed by the fighting around me to block his blade. Then Tong Rhongi appeared. He parried the dragon man's sword and sliced his knife across the man's neck. I finally freed my arm and fired at a dragon man running at Tong Rhongi. Tong Rhongi gave me a quick nod and stabbed another dragon soldier.

A flaming arrow arched overhead. Then hundreds of flaming arrows shot upwards and rained down into the trench. Thick, black smoke billowed up as fire raced through the trench. The screams of men caught in the fire soared above the roar of battle. It was a second wall of Greek fire. Like before, it split the dragon army in half.

Our bugles sounded. We began pushing the dragon men out of our defenses and toward the wall of fire. The dragon men fell back. We climbed over their dead to pursue them.

It was another two hours before every dragon soldier on our side of the wall of fire was dead or too injured to fight. The bugles sounded the retreat. I was exhausted but able to walk. I had been separated from Zhong, Mick and Simon during the fighting but had managed to stay with Tong Rhongi. We searched for our injured soldiers and bound their wounds. Then we carried or assisted them to the field hospital set up behind our defenses. Time was short. Once again, we left our dead where they fell. Preparing for the next attack was the priority.

BOOM! BOOM! BOOM!

We heard repeated explosions beyond the wall of Greek fire. Everyone expected incoming cannonballs and ducked instinctively, but the cannonballs never appeared. After twenty minutes, the explosions tapered off and then stopped.

"What was that?" I asked.

"The dragon army are advancing their cannons," Tong Rhongi said. "Their weight set off the deep mines. Come with me."

He led me to Shareef and the commanders. They were standing on a dune overlooking the defensive line, absorbed in an intense discussion.

Tong Rhongi took his position beside Shareef. I joined Mick and Simon, who stood behind Shareef. I did not see Zhong anywhere.

"Glad you survived," Mick said.

"I'm glad we all survived," I said. "Where's Zhong?"

"He is with his men," Simon said. "He prepares for the next attack."

We heard another series of booms from beyond the wall of fire. This time, they were followed by whistling sounds and cannonballs bursting through the fire. Most of the cannonballs hit the sand in front of our defenses and exploded. Some bounced until they collided with our defenses and either embedded themselves or exploded.

Fortunately, the wall of Greek fire blocked the dragon men from seeing us. Their cannons were firing blindly and were too far back to do significant damage. That would change quickly when the dragon army's spotters were able to see where the cannonballs hit.

Our cannons returned fire, but we were also firing blindly. The inability to see through the Greek fire worked both ways.

An hour after the dragon army's bombardment began, Mick leaned toward Shareef. "Sir, something's happening in the Greek fire."

Everyone looked where Mick pointed.

"I see nothing," Shareef said.

"Wait," Mick said. "It'll happen."

That is when we saw it: a sudden swirl at the bottom of the wall of fire.

"They're doing it everywhere!" the Jewish commander said.

I looked down the fire wall in both directions. The swirls appeared at one-hundred-yard intervals as far as I could see in both directions.

"Just as Zhong predicted," Tong Rhongi said. He nodded to a soldier waiting behind the sand dune with his bow and arrow. The soldier dipped the tip of an arrow into a campfire and then fired the flaming arrow into the air. It was answered immediately with booms and bangs as our cannons and gunfire peppered every swirl.

All the swirls stopped shortly after the bombardment began. Fifteen minutes later, the swirls reappeared in new locations along the fire wall. Our soldiers and cannons redirected their fire to the new swirls. When they did, the swirls disappeared and then reemerged in a different place. The pattern continued and sped up, until we were shooting at moving targets.

All Zhong's predictions were coming true. He had said the dragon men would fill the trenches with sand in preparation for their next attack. The first thing we would see would be swirls in the fire wall from tossed sand. When we fired into the swirls to stop them, they would shift their shoveling away from the barrage, and the swirls would appear in new locations in the wall.

Once the dragon soldiers partially filled a section of the trench, a permanent gap in the fire wall would appear. Spotters for the dragon cannons would use the gaps to increase their accuracy. With more sand, there would be bridges across the trench. Once the dragon army had enough gaps and bridges, their next attack would begin.

Zhong was suddenly beside me. "Shareef, the catapults are ready."

"Just in time," Shareef replied.

I was relieved to see Zhong. I didn't know where he had been, only that he had been supervising the final preparations for another of his proposals.

Zhong had supervised ten thousand soldiers in the building of four hundred catapults. Then he had trained the teams to operate them. The catapults were positioned at short intervals behind our entire line. I split my attention between the swirls in the fire wall and the catapult team closest to us.

The catapult spotter climbed the sand hill in front of the catapult to watch the wall of fire. The rest of the team inserted poles into holes in a large spool at the back of the catapult. They turned the spool and lowered a thick pole with a large bowl on the end until it was level with the ground. A soldier started a campfire while the others scooped black jelly from a large vat and filled the bowl. Then the team sat and waited.

Four hours after Mick pointed out the first swirl, a permanent gap in the wall of Greek fire appeared. I saw the face of a dragon man looking through the gap. He pulled back quickly when the barrage of gunfire began.

"We have a gap!" the spotter for the nearest catapult shouted. "Aim three degrees north!"

The soldiers swung the catapult slightly to the right. A soldier touched a torch to the campfire and then lit the black mixture in the bowl. Fire and black smoke appeared. A soldier released the catapult, and the bowl whipped forward with a loud thud. A flaming black mass hurtled skyward, trailing black smoke. The mass arched over and down, slamming into the gap with an explosion of fire. The gap in the Greek fire had been closed with more Greek fire.

Gaps in the wall of fire began to appear everywhere. The catapult teams responded quickly. THUD. THUD. THUD. The sounds were heard along our entire defensive line. They were followed by flaming black masses arching through the sky.

"Unbelievable!" Tong Rhongi shouted to Zhong. "To see two ancient weapons of war in a modern battle! This is beyond my wildest dreams!"

"This is the first time for me as well," Zhong said.

His comment was met by stunned silence among the commanders.

"You have never seen a catapult in action?" Tong Rhongi asked.

""No. And until we built them, I had never seen them."

"Then how could you build them?"

"I studied ancient parchments."

"Surely you have made Greek fire before," Shareef said.

"No. That knowledge also came from parchments."

Shareef, Tong Rhongi and the commanders burst out laughing.

"I'm glad you did not tell us this before," Shareef said. "I would not have allowed you to do any of this, and we would have already lost the war!"

Tong Rhongi put a hand on Zhong's shoulder. "Well done, my friend. You are truly Sun Tzu's greatest student."

Throughout the rest of the day, we kept up a steady barrage from our cannons, catapults and guns. Our efforts slowed the dragon army's attempts to shovel sand and build bridges across the trench, but we could not stop them. Their cannons pounded our defenses with increasing effectiveness, as their spotters continued redirecting their fire.

We were standing with the commanders on a sand dune, observing the situation. The sun had dropped below the western horizon, and the only light was the dark red glow of the fire wall. Cannon fire from the dragon army suddenly sputtered to a halt.

"They are almost ready for their next assault," Tong Rhongi said to Shareef and the other commanders. "We too should stop our barrage and use this time to prepare. The dragon soldiers will not stop their shoveling, but they are impossible to see. To fire blindly only wastes our ammunition and powder."

Shareef spoke to a messenger standing behind him. The soldier ran down the hill, and then I heard horses galloping to the north and south. A short time later, the barrage from our cannons, catapults and guns slowly stopped. In the silence of the cease-fire, we listened to the gritting sounds of dragon soldiers shoveling sand into the trench.

"Commanders," Shareef said. "It is time to return to your units. According to our scouts, the battle will resume with the first morning light. Use this time to care for our wounded. Repair our defenses. Distribute what remains of our ammunition and gunpowder. And lead your soldiers in prayer that their god will stand with us."

Mick, Simon and I were lying near the top of a defensive wall. Zhong had left to prepare his catapult teams for the coming attack. We stared into the blackness, our guns at our sides, waiting for dawn and the coming battle. We rotated who stood watch while the others rested. Knowing the battle was only hours away made sleep impossible. The sounds of the dragon men's constant shoveling added to our growing tension.

Someone shook my shoulder. "We're done sleeping, John," Mick whispered. "Something's happening!"

I was surprised to realize I had fallen asleep. I looked up and saw a thin dark-red line along the eastern horizon. The sounds of the digging had stopped. The intensity of the fire wall's red flames had diminished. It was too dark to see the sand bridges across the trench, but I knew they were there.

Then the dark outlines of shouting riders on horseback charged through the gaps in the fire wall and galloped hard across the sand bridges. Flaming arrows shot upwards into the black night. BOOM! THUD! BANG! Our soldiers unleashed a barrage of guns, cannons and catapults at the dragon cavalry. Dragon men and horses fell screaming from the bridges into the fiery trench. But the dragon cavalry kept coming. Each charge reaching closer to our defensive line before it was stopped.

When the dragon cavalry was within fifty yards of our position, more flaming arrows from our line arched upwards. Mick, Simon and I joined the soldiers leaving their positions to climb down the outside of our defensive wall. It was time to carry out another of Zhong's proposals. We all lifted long wooden poles hidden in the sand, rammed the blunt ends into the ground and aimed the sharp ends at the chests of the approaching horses.

The dragon horses were too close and moving too fast to halt or turn away. They ran straight into our spikes. The horses' momentum drove the points deep into their chests. All the horses writhed and screamed. My horse fell to the ground, crushing its rider and snapping the spike in my hands.

The dragon cavalry attack came to an abrupt halt, which rippled back through the charging horses to the cavalry crossing the sand bridges. Unable to advance, the dragon men and their horses were forced into the trench by the cavalry pushing forward behind them. The stench of burning flesh became intense.

Horns beyond the wall of fire sounded the dragon army's retreat. The flow of the dragon men and cavalry slowly reversed, as they fought each other to get back across the sand bridges. The fighting forced hundreds more cavalry into the fiery trench.

Our bugles sounded. Mick, Simon and I ran forward with a shout, knives and guns in hand. We fought our way to the nearest sand bridge, stepping on and over the bodies of the dragon men and horses and killed every dragon soldier in our path.

The battle was proceeding as planned. Our only chance to win the war was to inflict a decisive slaughter on the enemy, break their spirits and make them run back into the holes from which they had come.

Mick, Simon and I moved with the flow of soldiers. We had crossed a sand bridge and were inside a gap through the fire wall when I realized Simon was no longer with us. I kept glancing around me but couldn't see him.

When we stepped out of the gap, the rear of the retreating dragon army was forty yards ahead. They were trapped between their advancing army and our attack. We pushed into them, shooting and stabbing.

I saw blurs out of the corner of my eye and gave them a quick glance to confirm what I hoped.

Zhong was beside us with dragon men dropping all around him. The blurs were from his arms and hands. I was relieved to know he was there and fought with renewed energy.

After an hour of constant fighting, we were forcing the dragon men up a sand dune. I had used up my bullets and was stabbing and deflecting stabs with my knife. I was beyond exhaustion but couldn't stop. I kept moving by telling myself the battle had to end soon.

I finally reached the crest of the hill. My focus was on the dragon men directly ahead, but I could also see into the distance. We were at the edge of a vast sea of dragon soldiers that spread to the horizon. The scouts' reports about the size of dragon army had been wrong. The army wasn't huge; it was impossibly vast. For every dragon man we killed, a hundred more were ready to replace him.

All the soldiers on the hill saw what I did. Our will to fight drained away at the sight. Our efforts had been for nothing. There was no way to stop the prophet from reaching the third temple and awakening his god.

Our advance slowed and then halted. Sensing the shift in momentum, the retreating dragon men turned to face us. They gave a loud cry and charged, stabbing anyone they could reach, taking their revenge. Panic raced through our army. We turned and ran with a single thought: get through a gap in the fire wall and reach our defenses.

The crush of our soldiers forced me to the ground. I tried to push up onto my feet, but the bodies forced me back down and made me drop my knife. A dragon man appeared over me, his face twisted with rage. He stabbed at my face with a long knife. I grabbed his arm, but the knife kept edging closer. The tip of the blade had just touched my eye when the dragon man collapsed.

Zhong pulled me to my feet. "Stay behind me!" he said.

I followed him through the press of men. Somehow, Zhong brought us alongside Mick. He looked at us with the same exhaustion and hopelessness that overwhelmed me.

We were a hundred yards from the nearest gap in the fire wall with the dragon men close behind when a large golden man stepped through the flames. He was eighteen feet tall and stood with his face to the west. Simon was barely visible inside. The Golden Warrior had returned.

The dragon men fired at the Golden Warrior from all sides, but their bullets had no effect. The Golden Warrior/Simon nocked an arrow and aimed at the sky. They pulled back on the bowstring and released it with a loud thud. The arrow flew up until it was almost out of sight. It arched over and became a fiery ball trailing black smoke as it plummeted back to the earth. The fireball landed several hundred yards away inside the dragon army. BOOM! An explosion knocked everyone to the ground.

From where the fireball landed, a smoking fire sprang up and raced north and south. The flames cut a wide swath through the dragon men, killing tens of thousands and dividing the dragon army. The dragon men trapped on our side of the fire lifted their weapons and waited for the inevitable.

Once again, our army reversed direction and, with a roar, continued killing the enemy.

The sun was setting and every dragon soldier within sight was dead or dying. Our bugles finally sounded the ceasefire. Those of us who could walk began the search for our injured and bound their wounds. That accomplished, we half-carried them to the field hospital behind our defenses. The entire time Zhong, Mick and I worked, I looked for Simon but never saw him. He and the Golden Warrior had disappeared during the battle.

Having cared for the injured and carried them from the battlefield, we staggered to the command tent to find the others. The tent floor was covered with sprawling, snoring bodies. By the light of a kerosene lamp, we searched their faces for Simon, Shareef and Tong Rhongi. They were not there.

An Arab stepped into the tent and looked around. He spotted us and waved for us to follow.

"Please, Tong Rhongi requires your presence" he whispered.

"Do you know about Shareef and Simon?" Zhong asked.

"Yes. They are with Tong Rhongi."

The Arab led us to a tent surrounded by Shareef's Arabic soldiers. We followed our guide inside.

Shareef was lying on pillows with his eyes closed. His face and head were covered with dried blood and the dirt of battle. His breathing was rattling rasps, interrupted by flinches of pain. Tong Rhongi sat on one side of Shareef with a doctor holding a bloody bandage against Shareef's chest. Simon sat on the other side. He nodded to us and motioned for us to sit with them. I was horrified to see Shareef's injuries and relieved to see Simon. Unlike everyone else, he appeared untouched by the battle. His white hair and black skin were clean, and his robe was white.

"How bad is it?" Mick asked.

"A deep stab wound to the chest," Tong Rhongi said and then glared at the Arab. "His men were supposed to be guarding him."

"Sir, we were," the Arab said. "This happened during the retreat. The press of the soldiers separated us. A group of twenty dragon men reached the commander before we could. The commander killed six. We killed the rest."

The rasping of Shareef's breathing stopped.

Tong Rhongi placed a hand on his chest. "He lives, but his breath is shallow."

A horse galloped up to the tent. There was a short argument outside before a dusty soldier entered. He stood at attention and pulled a folded paper from inside his shirt. "A message for the commander!"

Tong Rhongi extended his hand. "Give it to me."

The soldier handed him the paper. "It comes from Al Aqabah."

"At the northern tip of the Gulf of Aqabah?" Tong Rhongi asked.

The soldier nodded.

Tong Rhongi read the paper with a frown. "This is a letter from this soldier's lieutenant. A ship arrived three days ago." He looked at the Zhong, Mick, Simon and me. "The ship's captain says he's there to meet you. He mentions you by name. This captain apparently does not know the purpose of the meeting but says that you do. So, what is this meeting?"

"I have no idea," I said, looking at my companions.

"What is the captain's name?" Zhong asked.

Tong Rhongi looked at the letter. "Paca."

"Paca?" Mick frowned. "He should be three hundred miles south of here."

"So, you do know the man?"

"He's a good friend," I said. "But there is no meeting, and we're not leaving."

Tong Rhongi crushed the paper in his hand and looked at the messenger. "Do you have anything else to tell us?"

"No, sir.

"It appears your long ride has been for nothing. When you return to your lieutenant, give this message: 'Commander Tong Rhongi says the men mentioned in your letter will not be coming.' Our men outside will show you where to rest and refresh yourself. I suggest you leave as soon as possible. We are about to engage in a deadly battle. You are excused."

The man looked confused as he bowed and left the tent.

"Tong Rhongi," Simon said, "my friends must board that ship."

"You heard them," Tong Rhongi said. "They are not leaving."

"If they do not leave, the war will be lost."

Tong Rhongi waved his hand dismissively. "Nonsense. A war is won or lost where the battle is fought! The battle is here!"

"As you yourself pointed out," Simon said, "even our victories weaken us. The Golden Warrior's wall of fire will soon burn out. When it does, the dragon army will attack and keep attacking until we are destroyed. Our only hope for victory is for my friends to leave now."

Tong Rhongi's eyes narrowed. "Is this from your special knowledge?"

"Yes."

"That means you, too, will leave."

"No. I remain."

"Then we still have the Golden Warrior!" Tong Rhongi said. "We can defeat them!"

"No, Tong Rhongi. I die soon after the next attack begins. The Golden Warrior dies with me. The destiny for which I was born is several hours away."

Tong Rhongi shook his head. "What kind of destiny is that? To die so evil will win? You must resist this destiny!"

"I did not choose my destiny, just as my friends did not choose theirs."

"Simon, we just can't leave," I said. "Not unless we have a reason, a good one. Otherwise it's nothing but desertion!"

"I'm sorry, John. I do not know the reason."

"I believe I do," Zhong said. "Tong Rhongi, may we speak privately?"

Tong Rhongi placed his hand on Shareef's bandage. "I will hold this, doctor."

The doctor and the Arab bowed and left.

Zhong spoke softly so the soldiers outside could not hear. "In the first temple, when the prophet was about to sacrifice my friends, he spoke about his god, he said it sleeps in a place called the Sanctuary. The Sanctuary is a monastery and my home. It is hidden in the Himalayan Mountains.

I was shocked that the prophet knew of these things. They are our greatest secrets."

"What is this god?" Tong Rhongi asked.

"His god is a large blue diamond called the Pathrokotau," Zhong replied. "The world and my friends know it as the Soul of the Beast. It has been with my people since before our earliest myth."

"Do your people worship this Pathrakotau?" Tong Rhongi asked.

"No. We are Buddhists. To us, it is just a diamond. I am the first of my people to know what it really is. The prophet also said John, Mick and I had begun his god's awakening. Thinking back, I knew he was correct."

"That was not our purpose," I said.

"It definitely wasn't," Mick said.

"So how did you begin this god's awakening?" Tong Rhongi asked.

"Again, sometime in the distant past, two diamonds had been cut from the Pathrakotau and carved into the shapes of an egg and a tiger," Zhong said. "We called them the Begotten. The two diamonds were stolen over five hundred years ago. We believed they were lost forever, until John's grandfather found them.

"John, Mick and I returned the carvings to the monastery. A monk placed them back in their original locations on the Pathrakotau. That is when a light in the center of the diamond began to beat. That act began the awakening of the dragon god."

Tong Rhongi nodded slowly. "Very interesting. But you have not told me why you should leave and board that ship."

"I believe the removal of the carvings forced the dragon god into its sleep," Zhong said. "The carvings must be removed to stop its awakening. Destiny has given us the task of removing the Begotten. The ship has come to take us to India."

Tong Rhongi quietly studied Shareef's pale face. "I have been to the Himalayas. It will take many days to reach them, even after you arrive in India. This war will be won or lost long before you reach your monastery. If your destiny is to stop the awakening of the dragon god, it can only happen here."

"Tong Rhongi, the chance that our friends can reach the monastery in time is very small," Simon said. "If they remain here, the loss of this war and the awakening of the dragon god are certain."

Tong Rhongi nodded, his eyes still on Shareef. "What you are saying, Simon, is a small chance is better than none."

"Yes."

"I know my commander would choose a small chance over none. If we cannot defeat the prophet and his army, we can at least delay them from reaching the third temple." Tong Rhongi looked at Zhong, Mick and me. "It appears our destiny is to die and buy you the time you need to reach the Pathrakotau."

Tong Rhongi turned and shouted. The Arab who had brought us leaped into the tent and came to attention. Tong Rhongi gave him orders in Arabic. The man bowed and hurried out.

"Horses and supplies will be here shortly. You will ride immediately to Al Aqabah. There will be fresh horses awaiting you when you need them."

"How are you going to do that?" Mick asked.

"That is my concern," Tong Rhongi said. "Yours is to ride as hard you can without stopping."

A soldier entered the tent and spoke into Tong Rhongi's ear. Tong Rhongi nodded. "Tell them I am coming. And ask the doctor to come back in."

The soldier ran out.

Tong Rhongi looked sadly at Shareef's face. "You were right, Simon, about the timing of the attack. The Golden Warrior's wall of fire is dying. Our scouts say the dragon army's attack is only minutes away."

CHAPTER TEN

We rode east at full gallop. Ahead was total darkness. Behind us were the bursting lights of intense battle. The bangs and explosions blended into a sputtering thunder. The dragon army attack had begun just minutes after we rode off. Tong Rhongi's final words to us had been to ride the Arabians hard and expect fresh horses before they collapsed.

"Behind you!" Zhong shouted.

Mick and I looked back over our shoulders.

A gigantic black dragon towered above the dragon army. Its eyes glowed blue. The edges of its body flickered with the red Greek fire. It was the dragon from the Valley of the Kings. Advancing toward the dragon, looking dangerously small in comparison, was the Golden Warrior. He held a shield out in front and his sword behind him. I could not see Simon, but I knew he was inside. Seeing the Golden Warrior entering the fight gave me a pang of guilt. Even though I understood the reason, I felt like a deserter.

The dragon spread its massive wings and lowered its head. It opened its jaws and spewed red-and-yellow fire. The Golden Warrior immediately tucked his head behind the shield. The fire flowed around him on both sides. He lifted his sword to strike and charged forward.

The two supernatural beings collided with an explosion of white light brighter than day. There was an ear-splitting crack followed by a blast of hot wind that made my horse stumble and almost blew me from the saddle. Blinded by the light and deaf from the sound, I held onto the saddle horn.

My hearing returned first. I heard the sounds of war and hooves pounding the sand below me. When my sight returned, I looked back. The western horizon was peppered with bursting lights. The Golden Warrior and the dragon were both gone.

Simon had been right about his destiny. He died sacrificing his life to a dragon, but not in the way he or the prophet expected. I prayed silently to Destiny. *If I am to die, let my death be as worthy as Simon's.*

We rode without stopping. The faint red of dawn was visible ahead, when my horse stumbled.

"We have to stop!" I yelled.

"There they are!" Zhong shouted.

On a hill directly ahead were the shadows of three riders on horseback and three rider-less horses. The riders dismounted as we approached.

We rode to the top of the hill and slid off our horses. My legs buckled beneath me, and I hit the sand. The men wore Bedouin robes and quickly transferred our supplies and rifles to the fresh mounts. Then hands pulled me to my feet and helped me onto my new horse. The Bedouins stepped away and bowed. We nodded our thanks and urged our new Arabians to a gallop.

"John! Mick!" Zhong pointed to the north. I shielded my eyes against the sun and saw a small cloud of dust. Riders were about to intercept us.

"Why is it never easy?" Mick shouted.

"What do we do?" I yelled.

"Keep riding!" Zhong said.

The riders were several hundred yards away when they opened fire. The bangs were followed by spitting sounds from bullets hitting the sand around us.

"Spread out!" Zhong shouted. "Together we make a large target!"

We urged our horses to the side and put twenty yards between us. The riders kept up their gunfire but never hit us or our horses. Mick and I fired back with our pistols and hit nothing.

The riders were less than 150 yards away before our Arabians' superior speed widened the gap between us. The riders continued their gunfire until we were more than three hundred yards ahead. That was when the riders stopped shooting and rode north and back to wherever they came from.

Realizing the riders could not have found us in that huge desert without help. I looked up, and there they were. Three dark spots circled high above us.

It was the third morning since we had started riding. The early light of dawn was an hour away. In the darkness ahead was a single light that I prayed was Al Aqabah. I had reached my physical limit and was fighting to stay awake and in my saddle.

We rode into a dark village at full gallop and headed straight for the light. I heard gunshots and then bullets hitting the walls around us.

We entered a small harbor. The light came from the dark outline of a ship at the end of a wooden jetty. We rode down the jetty and jerked our horses to a halt beside the ship. We threw our rifles and bags onto the deck and jumped aboard. Everyone went flat on the deck, and Mick and I readied our guns. The slow thumping of the engine sped up. I heard a churning of water behind the stern. A shadow crawled under the wheel and steered by holding the bottom.

Shadows ran onto the jetty and fired at the light. There were clangs and thuds as bullets hit near us. Two shadows jumped off the jetty and waded toward us. Mick and I fired, and our gunshots were followed by screams and groans.

Once we were three hundred yards from shore, the shooting stopped. The shadow at the wheel stood and relit the broken lantern hanging on the side of the cabin. The light revealed Paca's smiling face. "Seaman! Song! Meek! Joan!"

He stepped forward, and we stood to greet him. He gave us a crushing hug and then looked around. "Seaman?"

Our silence and faces told Paca that Simon was dead. Unable to speak his language, we couldn't explain the honor and purpose of his death.

Paca stepped inside the cabin and brought out a chart. He unrolled it on his chest with the blank side out. On the paper was the crude drawing of a woman with long hair and a long dress. Paca covered the drawing with his hand and pointed to the deck beside him. He pulled his hand away and pointed to the drawing and the deck. He looked at our faces, hoping we understood.

I shook my head. "I don't get it."

"I'd say there was a woman on his ship," Mick said. "Maybe it was one of Omar's women."

I looked at him. "Why would he tell us that?"

Mick shrugged. "I have no idea."

Paca covered and uncovered the woman and pointed at the deck three more times. From his frustration, the woman was obviously important.

"What if the picture is of a man?" Zhong said.

"That's it!" I said. "Simon's protector! He was on the ship!"

"And appearing and disappearing is what he does," Mick said.

Sensing we understood, Paca flipped the chart to the map side. He placed a finger on Al Aqaba, which we just left, then ran his finger down the Gulf of Aqaba to the Red Sea, around the Arabian Peninsula and east across the Arabian Sea to India.

"Simon's protector told Paca to take us to India," Zhong said.

I looked at the short distance between where the dragon army was now and the location of the third temple. I compared that to the long distance between us and India and then the distance across India before we could begin climbing the Himalayas. Tong Rhongi had been right. Our reaching the Sanctuary before the prophet reached the third temple was impossible.

Paca took hold of the wheel and gestured for us to lie on the deck. "Sleep!" he said.

We were too exhausted to do anything else. We nodded our thanks and found spaces between the woodpiles to stretch out.

As I drifted into sleep, my last thoughts were about the impossibility of reaching the Sanctuary in time and how our soldiers were dying to give us a chance. Our success or failure was not the issue. We owed it to them not to give up, not while we still breathed.

"Mick, John," Zhong said. "Wake up. It is time to resume our duties as crew."

Mick and I stood up. Zhong was at the wheel.

I couldn't see Paca and assumed he was sleeping in the cabin. I looked up. The crows were still there. "I hate those birds."

"We all do," Mick said. "Let's start with the boiler. I'll get the water. You get the fuel."

Mick pulled in a bucket of water while I carried an armful of fuel to the firebox. I passed by the cabin and saw a new crack in the porthole glass and fresh dents and splintered holes mixed in with the ones from our last trip with Paca. I was grateful to Paca for risking his life to save us, but I felt guilty that his reward was more damage to his ship.

Somehow we reached the Red Sea without seeing another ship. Three hours later, that changed.

Zhong, Mick and I were resting in the shade under the tarpaulin when Paca shouted, "Ship!" He pointed off the starboard bow to the west.

We could barely make out a thin line of smoke from a steamer.

"Dragon men?" Mick asked.

"With the crows watching," Zhong said, "that is likely. We shall know for certain in the morning."

The red light of early dawn had appeared in the east. Zhong, Mick and I were in the stern staring into the darkness. It was still too dark to see the ship, but we were close enough to hear the rapid chugging of its engine.

"It is a dragon ship," Zhong said.

I squinted at it. "Are you sure?"

"The ship sails at full speed," Zhong said. "A normal freighter conserves fuel. Dragon men do not."

"So, what do we do?" Mick asked.

"We continue as we are. When the dragon men come alongside, we will capture their ship."

"You make it sound so easy," Mick said.

"When the ship comes within the range of our rifles, top off the water in the boiler and fill the firebox one last time. Then shoot as many dragon men as possible. When the ship comes alongside, stop firing. Shoot only the dragon men who board our ship."

"Shouldn't we shoot them before they're on our ship?" I asked.

"I will be on their ship," Zhong said, "I do not wish to be shot."

The growing light revealed a two-stack steamer with thick black smoke pouring from both stacks.

When the dragon ship came within rifle range, Mick and I filled the engine boiler and the firebox. Paca tied the ship's wheel so it wouldn't turn and then hid inside the cabin. He popped his head up occasionally to look through the broken porthole.

We fired at the other ship and used the cabin for cover. The dragon men returned fire, but neither their shots nor ours came close. The rolling of the ships made aiming impossible. I hit one dragon man, but it was more luck than skill.

The fuel in our boiler ran out. The engine began slowing, and so did our ship. The dragon ship slid alongside us. It was twice the size of ours, and its deck was piled high with wood for fuel. More than twenty dragon men stood behind the wood for cover with their guns aimed at our ship. We stopped firing and kept the cabin between us and them.

The dragon ship reversed its engines and brought the decks of the two ships to within four feet of each other. Dragon men gathered at the edge of their deck. They watched the rocking of our ships and prepared to jump. The dragon men were such easy targets that it was difficult not to fire, but we did as Zhong asked.

Three dragon men jumped onto our ship. Mick and I fired as they landed and hit two of them. The third man threw himself behind the cabin. The dragon men on the other ship opened fire, and we pulled back. Mick touched my shoulder and pointed to the stern. I nodded, and he headed to the back. I kept watch for more dragon men.

I heard a gunshot in the stern, followed by a groan of pain. Before I could decide whether to check Mick or stay, another dragon man jumped. I shot him as he hit the deck. Another barrage of bullets came from the dragon ship. I pulled back, but not before I felt a sharp pain in my right shoulder.

The gunfire from the dragon ship stopped abruptly. I heard angry shouts and scattered gunshots and groans. I inched forward to peek around the cabin.

Three dragon men stood on the deck of the other ship, their rifles ready and their heads turning from side to side. Bodies covered the deck around them. One man's head jerked to the side, and he collapsed. The man beside him dropped to the deck. The last dragon man threw his back to the bulkhead and repeatedly fired at the bow and the stern before falling into a motionless heap.

"You keep hurting that shoulder," Mick said behind me.

"Just a graze," I replied, hoping it was true. "Did you get the dragon man?"

"He's dead."

Zhong appeared on the dragon ship's deck. He picked up a coiled line and began tying one end to a cleat. "John! Mick! I'm throwing you the line!"

"I'll get it," Mick said, stepping around me. He caught the line and pulled the ships closer before securing the line.

"Throw the guns and everything of use to this ship!" Zhong said. "Then come across!" He climbed the ladder to the wheelhouse and disappeared inside.

We threw our guns and anything else we could use to the dragon ship.

Paca came out of the cabin with an armful of rolled charts. He gave us a nod before jumping to the other ship. Still holding his charts, he climbed up to the wheelhouse with his free hand.

With everything we could use on the dragon ship, Mick undid the line from Paca's ship, and we both jumped across. As soon as my feet hit the other deck, the water behind the dragon ship's stern churned. The dragon ship, now our ship, began to move.

"Have a seat, John," Mick said. "I need to check that shoulder."

I sat on the deck with my back against a bulkhead. Mick filled a bucket with sea water. Then he eased me out of my shirt and rinsed my shoulder so he could give it a closer look.

"Good news is, it's not deep." Mick tore strips of cloth from the shirt of a dead dragon man and bandaged my wound. "Now if you could stop hurting your shoulder for a while…"

"I didn't do this to myself."

"I know," he replied. "Let's go check the engines."

We pulled back the aft hatch. At bottom of the hold were two steam engines. We climbed down the ladder and filled both fireboxes with wood and the boilers with water from the full buckets in the hold beside them.

Then we began the task of stowing the guns, food and other items we had thrown across from Paca's ship. That accomplished, we began the grisly task of searching the dead for money and valuables and then throwing them overboard.

As we dropped the first body over the side, I thought about the last time we did this. We were moving twice as fast as we had in Paca's ship. I was glad, because that meant, when the sharks arrived, we would be long gone.

We had rounded the southern coast of the Arabian Peninsula and were headed north. We had not encountered another ship, but it was just a matter of time. Our new ship put out three times more smoke than the old ship did. That meant we were visible from many miles away. But the smoke didn't endanger us or make us more visible than we already were. The crows were still overhead, making certain the prophet knew exactly where we were.

After tending to the engines and the boilers, Mick and I were sweaty and overheated. We doused ourselves with buckets of seawater and then joined Zhong in the shade of the wheelhouse. Zhong was looking to the north through a spyglass Paca had found in the wheelhouse. I followed the direction he was looking and made out a thin line of smoke.

"Here we go again," Mick said. "Another ship."

Zhong handed the spyglass to Mick. "Two ships."

Mick stared through the glass for a minute and then passed it to me. "Can we outrun them?"

"We'll know this afternoon," Zhong replied.

Mick and I kept the boilers brimming with water and the fireboxes full. Despite our efforts, the dragon ships drew closer. When the sun began its descent into the west, the two ships were three miles away. A puff of smoke appeared on the bow of the closest ship. It was followed by a boom, a whistle and a splash a hundred yards off our port bow.

Smoke puffs appeared almost simultaneously on both enemy ships, and the two splashes were closer than the first. The cannonballs hit nearer each time until they were twenty yards away, close enough for us to feel the spray.

Mick looked at Zhong. "What do we do?"

"The only thing we can. Continue as we are."

I almost cheered when the splashes that came after that were all slightly farther away than the one before. That meant our ship was faster than the dragon ships. We were starting to pull away.

Two hours later, the dragon ships ceased firing. I expected them to turn away, but they didn't. They just kept coming.

"They're not giving up," I said.

Mick pointed to the northeast. "There's trouble ahead, too."

Black clouds filled the horizon. Light flashed inside a cloud, followed seconds later by a deep rumble.

"A cyclone," Zhong said.

Mick sighed. "Just what we needed. Another disaster."

We did not need Paca to tell us. We began securing the ship for rough seas.

CHAPTER ELEVEN

We reached the port of Al Ashkharah at the same time as the black clouds. Lightning flashed around us with ear-splitting cracks. High waves and gusting wind rocked our ship. I looked up and couldn't see the crows. The storm had probably blown them away.

Al Ashkharah was on the edge of a barren desert. The only reason it existed was its location. It was the last place to refuel before sailing east across the Arabian Sea to India. It was also the first place to refuel when sailing west from India. Its importance to shipping had created a surprisingly large town with three long rock jetties.

The shoreline was thick with small ships and boats pulled as far onto the land as possible. Eight boats had already been claimed by the growing surf and were bouncing wildly in the waves. The town's streets were a mayhem of men, women and children struggling to pull down flapping tents and awnings and carry their wares to safety.

Zhong, Mick and I were with Paca in the wheelhouse. He eased the ship through the surf to a point forty yards from the shore. He had avoided the jetties, because the surf would have pounded our ship to pieces against the rocks. Paca turned the ship and aimed the plunging bow at the oncoming waves. He kept the engine running and used his hands to indicate I was to take the wheel and aim the bow toward the waves.

"John, Paca and I are going ashore to purchase the fuel and supplies we need to cross the sea," Zhong said. "You must watch for the dragon ships. They are not far behind us."

"Good luck getting the supplies," I said, my hands clutching the wheel.

Paca, Zhong and Mick climbed down to the deck. Watching for waves and dragon ships was difficult, because I could barely see anything. The world was in a dusk from the dark clouds, except for occasional bursts of lightning. Rain pelted the glass and covered it with a sheet of water. I had brief periods between waves to glance around for dragon ships and watch the others.

Paca, Zhong and Mick lowered the dinghy into the water with the hoist. Zhong and Paca stepped into the dinghy and then rowed to shore.

A minute later, Mick pulled the hatch open against the wind and slammed it behind him. "It's getting worse out there."

"With this weather, I doubt anyone's left to buy from," I said.

"Probably, but we have to try. We're down to five piles of fuel. Keep your eyes on the waves and watch for the dragon ships. I'll watch the shore."

Fifteen minutes later, Mick shouted, "Something's wrong! They're already coming back!"

I looked toward the shore. Zhong and Paca were running to the dinghy. They pushed it into the surf as dragon men poured out of the streets behind them. The dragon men shoved and knocked down everyone in their way. Paca and Zhong rowed hard, the dragon men wading into the surf and shooting at them.

"I'd better go down and help them," Mick said. He opened the hatch, climbed onto the ladder and slammed the hatch shut against the wind.

I kept glancing toward the dinghy but couldn't see it. After many long minutes, the hatch opened, and Paca stepped inside. He didn't bother shutting the hatch. He took hold of the wheel and advanced the throttle on the engines. I climbed down the ladder to help the others. I heard sporadic shots of gunfire. Zhong and Mick were fighting the wind and surf to hoist the dinghy onto the deck. I pulled on a line. The dinghy and the deck were both empty.

"What about fuel?" I shouted.

"Paca made other arrangements," Zhong said. "A merchant will meet us with fuel four miles to the north. But we cannot allow the dragon men to follow us. We are sailing east until we are beyond sight from the land. Then we will sail north to the meeting."

"He won't be there," I said. "You'd have to be crazy to go out in this storm."

Mick looked at me. "You mean like us?"

"The merchant gave his word," Zhong said. "He will be there."

We were offshore from the location of the meeting. Large swells rocked the ship and washed across the deck. I was shocked to see six camels bearing bundles and three men waiting on shore. The merchant had kept his word, despite the weather. Paca edged the ship as close as he felt safe before turning the bow into the waves.

I was behind the wheel again, struggling to see through the glass and steering into the waves. At Zhong's request, I was still looking for dragon ships, even though it was a waste of time. No one could have followed us in that storm.

Mick was with me in the wheelhouse and watching Paca and Zhong row through the choppy surf to shore. After twelve minutes of hard rowing, the dinghy reached the shore. Following quick bows, the men helped Paca and Zhong fill the dinghy with fuel and supplies and push the dinghy into the surf. Then Paca and Zhong rowed back to the ship. Mick climbed down to the deck to help unload the dinghy.

Zhong and Paca came alongside the ship and quickly threw everything up to Mick. Then they rowed back to shore. Mick opened the hatch to the hold and secured the wood and supplies inside. He closed the hatch and remained on deck. He held onto the ladder to keep his feet against a gusting wind and the slippery, heaving deck.

Zhong and Paca repeated the trip over and over for three long hours and had less than half of the supplies on board. The dinghy had just reached the shore for another load when Mick pulled open the wheelhouse hatch and, standing on the ladder, yelled inside. "John! Ships! Ring the bell! They have to come back now!" Mick slammed the hatch and climbed back down.

I put my face up to the rain-covered glass. Two hundred yards away, two large gray shapes were rocking up and down in the waves. Either they hadn't been there before, or I had missed seeing them the last time I looked. The smoke from their stacks blew sideways. Our ship was within easy range of their guns, but the rough seas made shooting impossible.

I pulled the rope for the ship's bell and kept it ringing it until Paca and Zhong looked toward the ships. They threw the fuel they carried into the dinghy and pushed it into the water. The three merchants led their camels into the desert.

It seemed like forever before Paca came through the wheelhouse hatch and took the wheel. "Song. Meek!" he said and pointed down.

I climbed down to the deck. Zhong and Mick were struggling to hoist the dinghy out of the water. It bucked and swung in the surf and the wind. I had just grabbed a line and pulled when a large wave slapped the dinghy and snapped the lines. Another wave flipped the dinghy hull-side up and drove it away from the ship.

"It's a loss!" Mick yelled. "John, let's fill the boiler before we go up!"

"I will help Paca," Zhong shouted and climbed up to the wheelhouse.

We cracked the hatch to the hold. Mick climbed down first. As I stepped onto the ladder, I paused. The gray shapes of the dragon ships were swinging up and down in the surf, closer than before.

After fighting the wind and the slippery steps, Mick and I threw ourselves into the wheelhouse. It took both of us to close the hatch against the wind. Paca was leaning over the wheel, straining to see through the glass. The ship was running at full speed, but the only motion I felt was the up and down heaving of the bow. Zhong was looking through a porthole toward the dragon ships.

Holding on to anything that wouldn't move, Mick and I crossed the deck to Zhong. I was shocked to see the dragon ships were only a hundred yards away.

"What now?" Mick asked.

"We sail to Bombay," Zhong replied.

"We don't have enough fuel," I protested.

"There is no choice."

A huge wave broke over the bow and rushed across the deck. Paca spun the wheel to the left and aimed for another large swell. He looked at us and frowned. "Bad!"

As we sailed deeper into the storm, the swells became small mountains, especially when looking up at them from the bottom. Large waves appeared out of nowhere, pounding the side of the ship and throwing us against the bulkheads. When we weren't being tossed around, Mick and I stared through portholes, looking for the dragon ships. The ships were gone. No one had seen them leave, but apparently, the storm had become too much for them.

"Meek! Joan!" Paca jabbed his finger straight down. It was time to check the engines.

Climbing down the wheelhouse ladder and crossing the deck was a fight against the wind and the waves. They kept trying to push us overboard. We never took a step without gripping at least one thing that couldn't move. Finally, we reached the rear hatch and climbed down inside.

I closed the hatch and we were in in total darkness except for the red glow of the fireboxes. Holding onto the ladder, we stepped into water above our ankles. Mick took a match from a watertight container and lit a candle from his pocket. The flame revealed bilge water sloshing up and down inside the hull, followed by an occasional hiss when the water sprayed onto the red-hot boilers. A full blast of water onto the boilers could cause an explosion. We had to lower the water level immediately.

Fortunately, we had the bilge pump. Mick had found it while we stowed the supplies. After our past experience, he thought we might need it and placed it near the ladder.

After filling the boilers and the fireboxes, we assembled the pump. I pulled a hose up the ladder, cracked open the hatch and fed the hose onto the deck. I closed the hatch as much as I could without clamping off the hose. Water still poured through the opening.

Mick attached the other hose to the pump and placed the end into the bilge water. We worked the pump handle as fast as our arms would move. An hour later, the water level was lower and less of a danger to the boilers. We sat in the water and rested our burning arms and shoulders.

After sitting for several minutes, we realized the water was creeping up our thighs. We had no choice but to resume pumping. The water coming through the hatch suddenly became a torrent.

Zhong was climbing down the ladder. He closed the hatch as far as he could. "Now I know what happened to you."

"And, as usual," Mick said, "we need help."

"We can rotate the work," Zhong said, taking my place on the handle. I filled the firebox and boiler before sitting and resting.

"We can't stop pumping, Zhong," I said, "If we do, the water level increases."

"I must leave periodically to relieve Paca. When I am with you, we will rotate the pumping."

"You'll be getting less rest than the rest of us," Mick said.

"We all do what we must," Zhong said.

On the third day out of Al Ashkharah, the storm had lost none of its fury. Zhong and I worked the pump, while Mick tended the boilers and fireboxes. He threw the wood into a firebox and slammed the grate.

"That's all of it," Mick said. "We're officially out of fuel."

"Now we use whatever burns," Zhong said.

"All right." Mick pulled an axe off a bulk-head. He began chopping the crates and anything else made of wood into pieces small enough to fit in the fireboxes. Now we had three tasks to rotate while Zhong was with us. When he left to relieve Paca, Mick and I worked the pump and ignored the engines except for quick refills of the boilers and fireboxes. We never rested.

Three days later, the crates were gone. Whoever wasn't manning the pump searched the ship for anything that would burn. We filled the fireboxes with broken-up barrels, sea chests, chairs and tables. Once those were gone, we used charts, coconut shells, books and even wooden spoons and a rolling pin from the galley. It gave us another two days of fuel. Once we exhausted those sources, we pried wood off the internal bulkheads and decks. That was good for five days of fuel.

On our twelfth day out of Al Ashkharah, all four of us were staggering and about to collapse from exhaustion. Mick and I had come to believe the storm would last forever. Zhong rarely mentioned it. The inside of the ship was now a cavernous space with a skeleton of supporting beams. The only remaining deck inside the ship was in the wheelhouse and under the steam engines.

Zhong had left to relieve Paca, and Mick and I were pumping out the water. After another quick break to fill the boilers and the fireboxes, my strength was gone. I dropped down in the water and sat against the outer bulkhead.

"Mick, I can't take this anymore."

Mick sank down beside me. "I'm definitely burned out."

"How about we take a little rest, and Zhong can wake us when he gets back? That wouldn't hurt anything, would it?"

"No, sounds good to me," Mick muttered.

Those words were the last thing I remembered.

Someone shook my shoulder. "John. Mick,"

"Sorry, Zhong," I mumbled and pushed myself up. "I couldn't help it."

Mick moved beside me. "My turn already?"

Zhong sat in the water beside us. "It's over."

"What's over?" I asked.

That's when I realized everything was strangely still. The only movement was the easy sway of the ship. Both steam engines were silent. The only sound was the lapping of water against the hull. A drop of water hit my head, and I looked up. The hatch was wide open. The sky above was blue with a mosaic of white clouds. A cool breeze brushed over me.

"Where are we?" Mick asked.

"Paca is figuring that out as we speak," Zhong said. "Come."

Zhong lay on the deck with Mick and me. We savored the luxury of doing nothing and soaking in the soft breeze.

"What a beautiful blue sky," Mick said. "And not a crow anywhere."

Paca climbed down from the wheelhouse and sat on the deck beside us. He unrolled a chart on the deck, and we sat up to look at it. Paca placed a finger on the chart. "Good!" he said.

Paca's finger marked a spot in the Arabian Sea just over one hundred miles from Bombay. If that was really our location, the storm had blown us farther and faster than we could have sailed without it.

"That's kind of hard to believe." I said. "Any chance Paca's wrong?"

"I don't think he is," Zhong said.

"If he's right," Mick said, patting the deck under us, "there's enough fuel to make it."

"Paca has a better plan," Zhong replied.

Paca pointed to the ship's two main masts. "Sail."

The sails were in the forward cargo hold and submerged in the bilge water. I had shoved the rolled-up canvas out of the way when we dismantled the inside deck. My thought was wet canvas wouldn't burn well. Fortunately, Mick and I didn't know about the wooden booms, spars and rigging inside the sails. If we had, we would have burned them along with everything else.

With Paca's guidance, we rigged the sails. As soon as we raised the main sail, it filled with wind, and the ship eased forward. With each sail we raised, the ship moved a little faster. After endless days of fighting to keep the engines going, it felt odd to sit and watch the wind do all the work.

Traveling by sail was slow compared to the engines, but there wasn't smoke to give away our presence. Twenty-eight hours after setting the first sail, we slipped unnoticed into the harbor of Bombay. I had never wanted to see India again, but I had never been happier to see any city in my life.

The harbor was three times busier and bigger than Calcutta's. Ships and boats were crowded two and three deep along the docks. Scum, oil, garbage and dead animals covered the water's surface. The hot humid air reeked of rot. Beyond the people swarming the wharves were run-down buildings and shops with shouting merchants

Zhong, Mick and I untied the lines holding up the sails and held them. As we approached the dock, Paca shouted out of the wheelhouse hatch, "Sail!" We released the lines, the sails dropped, and the ship began to slow. Paca steered the ship into a gap in the boats. When our bow nudged the wharf, Mick and I jumped onto the dock. Zhong threw us two lines, and we secured them to the pilings. After the harrowing trip through the storm, standing on something that didn't move was another strange experience.

Zhong joined us on the dock. "Stay here with Paca while I arrange for our transportation. Keep watch for trouble."

"From what?" Mick asked. "They can't know we're here."

"Do not be so certain," Zhong said. With those words, he melted into the crowd.

Mick and I climbed back on board. We pretended to be working while keeping an eye on the dock. We had rifles inside a nearby open hatch.

"I never thought we'd be here again," I said as I coiled a line

"And when did anything ever happen like we expected?" Mick asked.

Someone banged on the wheelhouse window. We looked up. Paca pointed at the wharf.

We stepped behind the wheelhouse, grabbed our rifles and peeked around the corner. The crowd on the wharf was oblivious to us, and everything looked normal.

"I wonder what he saw," Mick said.

I shook my head. "I have no idea."

The words had just left my mouth when an Indian man with a black beard and a purple turban emerged from the crowd. The purple turban meant he was a leader of the Indian assassin cult known as Thugs. They were the main reason I never wanted to see India again. They had tried to kill us and chased us from Australia to India and across India into the Himalayas.

"I thought they weren't looking for us," I whispered.

"Apparently, they changed their minds," Mick replied.

The Thug leader ran his eyes over our ship and snapped his fingers. Six Indian men without beards and turbans pushed out of the crowd and stood on both sides of him. They were the leader's servants, all of them trained killers. He and his men pulled guns and knives from inside their clothes.

"Here we go again," Mick whispered.

We lifted the barrels of our rifles and put our fingers on the triggers.

A Thug servant leaped onto the ship. I shot him as his feet hit the deck. The other Thugs opened

fire, a barrage of bangs and thuds, hitting the ship.
Then the gunfire sputtered to a stop. Thinking the
Thugs were about to charge, we pulled back, our
rifles aimed straight ahead. After a minute had
passed and nothing happened, I eased forward and
peeked around the corner.

The Thug leader and his men were collapsed on
the wharf with their necks bent at odd angles. The
crowd had pulled back, leaving an open area around
the bodies.

"Zhong?" I said. "You must be here somewhere."

"I am here."

I almost jumped out of my skin. Zhong was
standing right beside me.

"We must leave now." He waved up at the
wheelhouse. "Paca, come!"

The wheelhouse hatch burst open, and Paca
almost flew down the ladder.

We dropped our rifles to avoid attention and
then leaped onto the wharf. Shrill whistles from
constables sounded on the far side of the crowd.
Past experience had taught us that the constables
were not coming to help us.

Zhong led us into the crowd and away from
the whistles. The crowd scrambled out of our way.
Anyone seen with a Thug killer was as good as dead.
Mick did his best to make us less obvious by walking in a crouch. Moving at a near-run, we entered a
street heading away from the harbor. Like too many
Indian streets, it was packed with people, filth, shops
and merchants. I could not see the constables, but

their whistles were getting louder which meant they were catching up.

Moving as fast as the crowds allowed, Zhong took us through a maze of alleys and streets, slowing only when Paca fell behind. I was relieved when the constables' whistles grew fainter. It was only when we no longer heard them that Zhong slowed to a normal walk.

An hour after leaving the ship, Zhong stopped and opened a door. He waved us into a small windowless building. He shut the door behind us, and we were in complete darkness. I heard a latch sliding shut.

"We are safe," Zhong said.

I sat on the hard-packed dirt floor. There was a scraping sound, followed by orange-red sparks. A small blue flame appeared at the top of a candle. The light grew, revealing Zhong's face and then a small empty room with bags in a corner.

Zhong handed a water bag to Paca. He took a flatbread from another bag and broke off pieces for all of us.

"Lucky for us, you came back when you did," Mick said.

"It was not luck. The monk I met to arrange our travel said the Thugs were watching the harbor and the trains for us. I returned immediately."

"I thought the Thugs had stopped looking for us," I said.

"They did," Zhong replied. "Up until two weeks ago. That is when the Thugs received a message from the prophet. He ordered the Thugs to watch for us at the harbor and the trains. They were to kill us when the saw us."

Mick shook his head. "There's two problems with that. Thugs don't take orders from strangers. And how could a message get here faster than we did?"

"I have been considering the same questions," Zhong said. "We know the Thugs worship Kali. If the dragon god and Kali are the same, then the prophet is not a stranger. He is their spiritual leader."

"Did you mention this to the monk you met?" I asked.

"Yes. He knew nothing about the Pathrakotau's awakening or a connection between the prophet and the Thugs. He did know the Thugs have been receiving messages from Africa. It was after a message that the Thugs began watching the harbor and the trains. That message arrived a short time after we escaped the first temple."

"Assuming you're right," I said, "how could the prophet know we're coming to India when we didn't even know?"

"Just as Simon's magic told him things," Zhong replied, "perhaps the prophet's magic told him. The how is not important. What matters is the Thugs knew and they were watching for us.

"I learned something else from the monk," Zhong continued. "There is a constant relay of information between monks in the world and the

Sanctuary. One week ago, all contact with the Sanctuary stopped."

"What does that mean?" I asked.

"The monk did not know."

"Sounds like we're too late," Mick said, "and the dragon god's already awake."

"We cannot assume anything," Zhong replied.

Someone knocked lightly on the door. Mick and I jumped to our feet. Our first thought was the Thugs had found us.

Zhong unlocked the door, and an Indian man entered. He bowed and sat beside Paca, and the two men began talking.

"Who's he?" Mick asked.

"His name is Parmod," Zhong replied. "He is a friend. He is telling Paca that the ship that brought us here is now his. Fuel and supplies are being loaded. Parmod and another man will be his crew. Paca's destiny is to return to Africa. Ours is to continue on."

After speaking for a few minutes, Parmod and Paca stood. We stood, too. Paca looked at us sadly and said something to Parmod.

"Paca wishes to remind you that you are now his brothers," Parmod translated. "He would not leave if it was not his destiny."

Paca hugged us with tears in his eyes. "Sung. Meek. Joan." His hugs were surprisingly gentle. Then Parmod and Paca bowed and hurried out.

"That was fast," Mick said.

"We, too, are leaving," Zhong said, handing us the bags. "Our train departs in thirty minutes. Mick, I must ask you to slouch again."

Zhong led us through another labyrinth of streets and passageways. We halted at the edge of an open square with a large railway station. The station's architecture was overly ornate and typically British. It clashed with the brick-and-mud buildings that made up the rest of the square. Hundreds of people passed in and out of the station's main entrance. Hundreds more stood on a long raised platform behind the station.

Four trains waited on four sets of tracks behind the station. Thick black smoke poured from the stack of the engine alongside the platform. The engine's whistle gave a long blast followed by three short blasts.

"Our train is leaving," Zhong said.

He led us around the end of the station. We stopped where we could see the platform without being detected. Standing in the middle of the platform were six Indian men, including one with a purple turban. The men watched all approaches to the trains. There was no way to reach our train without being seen.

Mick shook his head. "Like I said, nothing's ever easy."

Zhong closed his eyes. A moment later, a Thug spoke to the leader and pointed to the far end of the platform. The leader shouted, and all the Thugs ran to the other end, shoving people out of their way. Zhong seized the moment to lead us past the platform and between two freight cars.

"Last call!" a conductor shouted. "All aboard!"

The engine's steam whistle blew two long blasts, and the train began to chug forward. Zhong slid back the door of a freight car. We threw our bags inside and climbed up. The car jerked hard and began to roll forward. Zhong closed the door.

The only light and air came through grated vents high on the side walls. The floor was filled with stacks of crates and piles of bulging burlap bags. Zhong led us through a tight gap between the crates to a small open area with a pile of blankets and bags. We sat silently on the wooden floor.

"It is now safe to speak," Zhong said.

"So, where are we heading?" I asked.

"Gorakhpur, near the base of the Himalayas. It is a five-day journey."

"And what do we do for five days?" Mick asked.

Zhong leaned back against a crate. "We rest. It appears Destiny has answered your wish for something easy."

I turned to Zhong. "You said Parmod was a friend. What did you mean?"

"Monks have many friends throughout India and the Himalayas. Parmod is one of those friends."

"I thought monks tried to be invisible," Mick said. "Friends should be the last thing you want."

"We have many tasks we could not accomplish without them. They help us and we help them in return."

"I'll bet the friends don't know you the way we know you," Mick said.

Zhong nodded. "No, they do not. Our friendship is unique. You are the only friends who know all of our secrets."

With nothing else to do, we surrendered to the fatigue that had been building in us for weeks and slept for two full days. Once we were rested, we spent our time eating, talking and standing on the crates and staring through the vents at the passing trees, farms, huts and villages.

The only breaks from the monotony were when the train stopped to load and unload freight or switch cars. Our freight car's door was opened at most of the stops. Men grunted and cursed as they lifted crates and bags in and out. At those times, we remained silent and motionless inside our open area until after the train began moving again. I noticed the men never touched the crates around us. I never asked, but I knew why. Zhong used his mental control to keep everyone from our crates.

On the morning of the fifth day since boarding the train, the air was distinctly cooler than when we boarded the train in Bombay. The Himalayan Mountains were visible through the vents. They looked like rows of grey, jagged teeth crowned by white. Some of the peaks were lost in white clouds.

"We are twenty miles from Gorakhpur," Zhong said. "It is almost time to jump. We must prepare."

We stuffed our remaining supplies into the bags. Mick slid the freight car door to the side, and we stood in the opening, watching trees, fields and huts slide past.

"It is almost time," Zhong said. "Roll when you hit the ground. When you stop rolling, do not move until I say."

I was shifting my bag on my shoulder when Zhong said, "Jump!"

We jumped.

I hit the ground hard. The impact knocked the air out of my lungs and tore the bag from my hands. I did not have to try to roll, because I couldn't stop rolling. When I did stop, I remained as still as a stone. Out of the corner of my eye, I watched the train until it was out of sight.

Several minutes later, Zhong whispered, "Gather your things."

He led us at a fast walk along the tracks in the direction of the train. When a village came into view several hundred yards ahead, we left the tracks and entered the woods on the side of the mountains. We paralleled the tracks, using trees and brush for cover, until we reached a path. We followed it toward the Himalayas.

After hiking for several hours, the path entered a small clearing with a single hut. The hut made one side of a corral constructed from wooden poles. Inside the corral were three Mongolian horses, saddled and ready to ride. Tied to their saddles were supply and water bags, rifles, thick gloves and parkas with hoods. This was exactly like what happened after we had first met Zhong. I had wondered then how he had arranged for the horses to be ready. Now I knew.

"I assume one of your friends did this," I said.

Zhong nodded. "Yes."

Like the first time, we rode single file out of the corral, with Zhong in the lead. The path that had brought us there continued on the far side of the clearing. Still heading toward the mountains, we entered the path and urged our horses to gallop.

CHAPTER TWELVE

Once we reached the foothills of the Himalayas, the path became steadily steeper. Eventually, we had to slow our horses to a walk. At this point, the mountains loomed above us. We had to crane our necks backwards to see the peaks.

"Thugs!" Zhong said, pointing behind us.

On the slope far below us was a line of barely visible specks. I looked up, expecting to see circling crows, but the sky was clear, except for a few scattered clouds.

"I already looked," Mick said. "No crows."

"Then how did they find us?"

"How they found us changes nothing," Zhong said. "What matters is they did."

We rode without stopping for the rest of the day, keeping one eye on the Thugs behind us. The increasing steepness of the mountain soon forced our horses into a slow, trudging climb. Whenever I looked back at the Thugs, they were always there.

As the sun descended below the mountains, the light grew dim and our horses began to stagger and slip on the rocky surfaces. We should have rested the horses, but the Thugs weren't stopping, and that meant we couldn't stop either. When Thugs hunted human prey, they didn't stop until they caught them. We knew this from our previous time in India. The Thugs took a drug to eliminate their need for sleep and rest. They also gave the drug to their horses to keep them moving.

The sun was almost completely below the mountains when an icy wind sprang up. The temperature plummeted below zero, and we pulled on our parkas and gloves. The sun finally dropped below the mountains and seemed to take the light with it. We were suddenly in complete blackness, except for the myriad of stars overhead.

A line of torches appeared behind and below us. We couldn't risk a torch. If the Thugs got close enough to shoot us, the torch would give them a target. We had no choice but to ride blindly through the dark, with Zhong leading. Mick and I lined up behind him and kept our horses' noses against the horse ahead. Zhong had found his way forward through darkness many times before. We trusted him to do it again.

After a night I thought would never end, the dark red of dawn appeared on the eastern horizon. The mountains slowly materialized in the darkness. The snow covered peaks and the surrounding clouds had a pink-orange hue in the early light.

We were beyond exhaustion. Our horses staggered with each step. Mick and I were battling to stay awake. We kept drifting into sleep and startling awake just before falling from our saddles. Our breath and the breath of our horses came out like white smoke. Crusts of ice had formed on our mouths and noses.

It was after a near fall from my saddle that I noticed something odd about one of the mountains. It took a while for my sleep- and oxygen-deprived brain to recognize what was wrong. A gray-black cloud surrounded the top of a mountain and rose high above the other peaks. It was an erupting volcano. I knew without doubt it was the mountain of the Sanctuary. That explained why contact with the Sanctuary had ended abruptly. I couldn't help but think the volcano meant the dragon god had already awakened, and we were too late.

Mick looked back at me and shook his head. He, too, had seen the volcano and had the same thoughts. Zhong kept his eyes straight ahead and said nothing. I knew he had seen it. He saw everything.

A half hour later, Zhong halted us behind a small hill. The horses were stumbling even when standing and frothy with sweat. We had to rest them or lose them. We gave them water in our cupped hands and let them graze on the sparse grass. We climbed to the top of the hill and huddled together for warmth. We ate while watching the Thugs. I was shocked to see how close they were, so close I could make out the individual riders.

"We know you saw the black cloud," Mick said. "Is that what we think it is?"

"The volcano of the Sanctuary has erupted," Zhong replied. "But we must not assume anything else."

I shivered. "I'd still like to know how they found us."

"The prophet is following us through his magic. He knows our destination is the Sanctuary. When he told the Thugs to find and kill us, he gave them the location of the Sanctuary. The Thugs simply positioned men on all routes leading to the mountain and waited for us to arrive."

"How do you know this, Zhong?" I asked.

"There is no other explanation."

"Well, we obviously can't outrun them," Mick said, looking down at the Thugs and taking a bite of bread, "Any alternate routes we can take to lose them?"

Zhong nodded. "There are several, but, with the volcano, they may not be open. Even if they are, they would take far too long. We must continue as we are. If an opportunity presents itself, we will use it. If one does not appear, there is a last possibility."

"So, you do have a plan," I said.

"It is more of a last option."

Mick crawled backwards down the hill. "I'd say it's time to get the horses."

We were climbing an ice-covered ridge when the icy gusts became a steady wind. It pushed us back down the mountain, almost as if it was helping the Thugs. After an hour of riding into the wind and slipping with every step, our horses stopped and refused to move. We had no choice but to dismount and reduce the weight on their backs. The horses let us lead them by the reins. Our pace was agonizingly slow as we slipped along with them, but at least we were moving. I looked back periodically. Each time I did, the Thugs were closer.

We were halfway up the ridge when we heard the echoing bangs of gunfire. Bullets pinged and ricocheted off the rocks behind us. The only cover was a heap of rocks a hundred yards ahead. We pulled on the reins to make the horses move faster, but they pulled back and wouldn't take another step. I yanked harder on my horse's reins, and he reared.

"Leave the horses! "Zhong said. "We must reach the rocks!"

It was a waking nightmare. Running and slipping with every step. The echoing bangs and pinging of bullets hitting closer and closer.

We were twenty yards from the rocks when Mick yelled and dropped, grabbing his left ankle.

Zhong and I each grabbed one of Mick's arms and pulled him forward. Mick hopped on his good ankle. Panting and exhausted, we threw ourselves behind the rock pile. Zhong checked Mick's ankle while I watched the Thugs. I ducked every time I heard a gunshot.

Mick's boot had a hole and a dark, wet stain. Zhong took hold of the boot. "This will hurt."

"Just do it!" Mick hissed through clenched teeth.

Zhong yanked the boot off, and Mick groaned. Zhong rolled down Mick's bloody sock. "The wound is superficial."

I lifted my coat against the cold and tore two strips of cloth from my shirt. Zhong used them to make a pressure bandage and pushed the boot back onto Mick's foot. Mick grunted in pain.

I edged my head up to see over the rocks. Gunshots echoed down from somewhere above us. We went flat as a barrage of bullets pinged around us. We were pinned down by Thugs above and below. Our situation was impossible.

"I hope this doesn't wreck your back-up plan!" Mick yelled over the gunfire.

"From here on, you must trust me," Zhong said. He shouted toward the Thugs above us. "Do not shoot! I wish to trade for our lives!"

The shooting slowed and then stopped.

"Your lives are mine!" an angry voice yelled down. "And I shall have them!"

"Let us live, and I will take you to the Soul of the Beast!"

There was a short silence. "Your words mean nothing to me."

"My words mean everything to you! You know all about of the Soul of the Beast and the powers it grants its possessor, and I know exactly where it is. I will take you to it, and you will receive all the powers the Soul of the Beast has to give. You will be the greatest of men!"

There was another pause. "No more talk! Throw down your weapons. Step out to where I can see you!"

Zhong sent his gun clattering across the ice.

"Don't do this, Zhong!" I whispered. "We're dead anyway. Make them come to us! We'll at least take some of them with us!"

"We must reach the Soul," Zhong whispered. "We must do it quickly." He raised his hands and stepped out from behind the rocks.

A Thug wearing a parka stood up from behind rocks above us. A purple turban was visible through the opening in his hood. "I will listen to your nonsense, but be quick!"

"I know the location of the Soul of the Beast," Zhong said, "and how to reach it. Spare our lives, and I will take you to it."

"I've heard enough!" the Thug leader shouted. "Come out, English! Now! Or I shoot your Chinaman!"

Our hearts pounding, Mick and I tossed out our guns.

"If this is the back-up plan, it stinks," Mick whispered.

We raised our hands and stepped into the open beside Zhong.

Six Thugs stood with their rifles aimed at us, three on each side of their leader. They followed him down the ridge and stopped fifteen feet away. Like us, ice covered their mouths and noses.

"I do not believe you, Chinaman," the leader said. "You would say anything to save your precious lives."

"Then believe your eyes." Zhong pointed to the black cloud. "The Soul of the Beast is inside that volcano. You are that close to immortality and all your dreams. Let us live, and I will take you to it."

The Thug leader looked at the volcano. "I need only one guide, Chinaman. Kill the English."

I heard clicks as the Thugs cocked their rifles.

"If my friends die," Zhong said, "so will you and your men."

The leader smirked. "You cannot threaten me, Chinaman."

"I do not threaten."

The Thug studied Zhong for a moment. "Know this, Chinaman, I, too, do not make threats. You will give me the Soul of the Beast, or you and the English will die slowly, with much pain."

Keeping the rifles aimed at us, the Thugs surrounded us. They pulled our hands behind our backs and tied them together. Then they put their hands on our shoulders and forced us to our knees.

The Thug leader stepped to where he could look down at us. He nodded. Rifle butts clubbed the back of our heads and knocked us to the ground.

The leader sniffed. "That is for not dying at the ship."

Panting and leading their horses and ours by the reins, the Thugs from below us arrived and then collapsed. Their ice-crusted faces showed surprise and then anger and confusion at finding us alive. While his men rested, the leader talked to them and pointed repeatedly to the volcano. His men looked at the black cloud with blank faces. They had to be questioning their leader's sanity for wanting to enter an active volcano but said nothing. To question him meant instant death.

The leader stopped talking. His men stood and formed the horses into a single-file. They untied our hands and then retied them in front. Rifle barrels jabbed our backs as they herded us to our horses. We took their reins and were prodded to our positions in the line. Zhong and his horse were behind the leader at the front of the line. Mick and I were positioned in the middle of the line. The Thug leader shouted, and the column started forward, everyone leading the horses by their reins. Mick was one Thug ahead of me. He limped with every step.

After three hours of trudging, we reached the top of the icy ridge. The terrain ahead was still icy but not as steep. The leader shouted, and the Thugs mounted their horses. Mick and I didn't move fast enough to suit our guards, so they jabbed their rifles into our backs. Mick winced as he swung his injured ankle over his horse's back. Then the column moved forward at a trot.

We rode until the sun began its drop behind the mountains. When it was too dark to continue, the Thugs halted and dismounted. They lit torches and drank from the water bags. They watered all the horses, including ours, with cupped hands. Then the Thugs pulled out small bags from inside their shirts. They opened them and poured a powder into their hands. It was the drug that eliminated their need for rest.

The Thugs swallowed half and then held the rest up to the horses' muzzles. The Thugs didn't offer anything to Mick or me. I didn't want the drug, but I did need the water.

We remounted and we rode at a slower pace, the fluttering torches lighting our way. The drug had eliminated the Thugs' need for rest, but Mick and I were still fighting our losing battle against sleep.

The Thugs took their first true rest near noon the next day. Mick and I fell from our saddles to the ground. When the Thugs dropped from their saddles, they staggered slightly, which I enjoyed. The Thugs ate, drank, swallowed more powder and then tended to their horses. Like before, they gave nothing to Mick or me. We huddled together beside our horses, using them to block the wind. We tried to ignore our thirst and hunger but it was impossible.

I was startled awake by a touch on my arm.

"Talk quietly," Zhong whispered.

He was sitting beside us with his hands tied in front like ours. I glanced at the Thugs, expecting them to club us with their rifles, but they continued eating and drinking, completely unaware of Zhong's presence.

"Do not worry," Zhong whispered. "They cannot see us. They see you as still sleeping." He handed Mick a water bag. Mick took four long swallows before handing it to me.

"What about their leader?" Mick asked.

"He sees me meditating beside my horse. How is your ankle?"

"Still hurts," Mick said, "but not as bad."

I shook my head in disbelief. "I don't understand, Zhong. If you can control their minds, why aren't we escaping right now?"

"Yeah, why did we even surrender?" Mick asked.

"If we try to escape, the situation becomes very complicated. My ability to control their minds is limited by the drug and their exhaustion. I cannot control them all at the same time. The Thugs I do not control could kill both of you. By using the

246

Thugs to take us to the Sanctuary, we will get there faster than we could on our own. You must trust my judgment."

"Sorry to doubt you," I said. "It helps to know what's happening."

"We are about to leave." Zhong picked up the empty water bag.

"And just for the record," Mick said, "is this the back-up plan?"

"Yes, this is the back-up plan."

We were crossing a ridge that took us beneath the black volcanic cloud. The daylight immediately turned to dusk. The air was thick with smoke and the stench of sulfur. Ash began covering the Thugs, the horses and us. After riding five miles under the black cloud, the ridge ended at the base of a cliff. The cliff was five hundred feet tall with a narrow gash that ran from the top to the bottom. I watched the leader ride into the gash without hesitation. Zhong was right behind him. The rest of the Thugs followed without slowing, but they whispered anxiously to each other. We were now riding inside the volcano, and they didn't like it.

When it was my turn to enter the cleft, I found myself at the bottom of a narrow gorge with vertical walls. If my hands hadn't been tied, I could have touched both walls at the same time.

As the gorge wound into the mountain, the air grew warmer and thickened into a fog. Soon, everyone was sweating and pulling off their coats and gloves. With our hands tied, Mick and I pulled the coats over our heads with our hands and then pushed them down our arms with our heads.

We had been riding for at least an hour when the walls of the gorge moved apart and seemed to disappear into the fog. Large, tall shapes, like gray ghosts, towered above us on both sides. I sensed wide open areas beyond the shapes on both sides. I couldn't see them through the fog and didn't know what they were. When I was close enough to touch a shape, I felt thick ash and pine needles.

The leader shouted, and the Thug column sped up to a gallop. Branches brushed against me. I lowered my head to my horse's neck to keep from being swept off. After ten minutes of hard riding, a second cliff seemed to jump out of the haze. The column came to a sudden stop. The Thugs dismounted and began removing the bags and weapons from the horses. Mick and I dropped from our saddles and collapsed to our sides. We were too tired to even sit.

Our Thug guards stepped toward Mick and me with their knives out, and we immediately sat up. I braced for a blade to my chest or neck. Instead, they pulled us to our feet, cut the ropes off our hands, pulled off our coats and then retied us. Our arms were loaded with bags, and I sighed with relief. They weren't going to kill us, at least not yet.

The Thugs lined up in single file. Their leader stepped up to the cliff, Zhong still behind him. They both appeared to disappear into the stone. Then the line of Thugs passed into the stone. It wasn't until I was closer that I saw the opening of a cave. I hesitated before stepping into the blackness, and a rifle butt knocked me inside.

CHAPTER THIRTEEN

The air inside the cave was ten times hotter than the warm air outside. It had an intense sulfur stench that burned my eyes. I followed the line of Thugs and shuffled forward in the pitch blackness. The line stopped moving, and a speck of light appeared in the darkness ahead. The leader had lit a torch and used his torch to light the torch behind him. The second torch lit the one next in line. The flame flowed toward me and then past me as the pattern repeated. Soon, the tunnel was filled with flickering yellow-orange lights and shifting shadows. We were in a volcanic tunnel with the same diamond-hard black stone walls we had seen inside Mount Tadjoura.

The line of Thugs started forward. I started at the same moment as the Thug ahead of me, but the guard behind me still clubbed me in the back. We sped through tunnels that twisted back and forth and up and down but mostly up. Mick was still staggering on his injured ankle.

After what felt like hours, the Thugs halted and sat. Mick and I dropped to the ground. We watched as the Thugs ate and drank and, as usual, offered us nothing.

Suddenly, Zhong was sitting beside Mick with a finger to his lips to indicate silence. He gestured for me to move closer. The Thugs around us, including our guards, were oblivious to Zhong and my movement.

Zhong felt Mick's ankle through his boot.

Mick winced. "It's okay," he whispered.

"Any other problems?" Zhong asked softly.

"Nothing food and water wouldn't help."

The Thug guarding me suddenly extended his arm alongside me. I jerked away to avoid a blow. Instead, he dropped a large piece of bread in my lap. I tore the bread into three pieces and passed them out. The Thug guarding Mick dropped a water bag in his lap. Mick took several long swallows and then passed the bag to Zhong.

Zhong took a long drink and then handed the bag to me. "The Thugs believe they are sharing their water and bread with each other," he whispered. "Drink all the water, but do it quickly. This will not be a long rest."

I emptied the water bag.

"Give it back to Mick's guard," Zhong said quietly.

I held the bag in front of the Thug. He took it and muttered angrily.

"What did he say?" I asked softly.

"He called your Thug a pig," Zhong whispered.

"I can agree with that."

"Any chance to escape yet?" Mick asked softly.

"Soon. You must watch me at all times. When I act, do exactly what I do. It is time for us to return to our positions."

Zhong disappeared, and I slid back into my spot. A minute later, the Thug leader shouted. Mick and I stood up with everyone else. That did not stop our guards from clubbing us.

It felt like we had hiked for hours through endless tunnels. I tried to keep Zhong's head in view. Most of the time, I couldn't see him because of the turns in the tunnel and the long line. I began watching Mick's head instead, hoping he could see Zhong.

A turn in the tunnel gave me a rare view of Zhong's place. He wasn't there, and my stomach almost jumped into my chest. I looked for Mick and saw him move to his right and out of sight. As the line moved past the spot, the opening into a small side tunnel appeared beside me. I jumped inside and took three quick steps before running into an upright body that had to be Mick.

The torches in the main tunnel made me visible to anyone who looked into our tunnel. I felt dangerously exposed. I kept expecting someone to grab me, but nothing happened. The Thugs trudged past our tunnel without a glance. Zhong had to be controlling their minds.

The last Thug walked past. Complete darkness followed in his wake. The echoing sounds of footsteps faded and finally disappeared. I felt a knife cut the ropes around my wrists. Then several unlit torches were placed in my hand.

That should have been the moment when we ran as fast as we could through the small tunnel and away from the Thugs. Instead, I heard the scraping of Zhong's flint and saw a shower of sparks. An orange-red flame spread over the head of a torch and revealed Zhong's face. It made no sense. The torchlight was a beacon in the darkness. If I didn't know better, I'd say Zhong wanted the Thugs to find us.

"Shouldn't be leaving?" I whispered.

"Not yet," Zhong said softly.

A minute later, we heard echoing shouts and the rapid thudding of feet running toward us.

"Run!" Zhong whispered, and we ran, his torch leading the way.

We were finally doing what we should have done minutes earlier. The shouts and footsteps grew louder when the Thugs entered our tunnel. We had just reached the junction of three tunnels when we heard a bang. I heard a ping beside me, and a rock fragment stung my face. Zhong led us into the left opening without hesitation. The sounds of the Thugs grew fainter and then louder as they entered our next tunnel.

After that, we raced through a long series of tunnel junctions. The only time Zhong slowed the pace was when the sounds of the Thugs grew faint. When their sounds grew louder, we would run again. This made no sense. I hoped Zhong knew what he was doing, because he was taking us, and the Thugs, deeper into an impossible maze.

After hours of endless tunnels, and the repeated slowing when the sounds of the Thugs became faint and running when they were loud, we reached another fork. The sounds of the Thugs had disappeared in the last tunnel, and I expected to slow down or even stop. But Zhong immediately led us into another tunnel and kept us running. The relief was a weight off my chest.

When we entered a large cavern, it had been an hour since we had last heard the Thugs.

Zhong lifted a hand for us to halt. "It is safe to rest."

Panting, Mick and I collapsed on the stone floor.

Our last torch was sputtering. I was expecting to go back into complete blackness when Zhong reached behind a rock. He pulled out an armload of fresh torches and two bags. He lit a new torch, placed it in a crack in the floor, then handed a water bag to me.

I took a long swallow and then passed it to Mick. "How did you know this was here?"

"My people have kept supplies at this place for centuries."

Mick swallowed and wiped his lips. "For what?"

"We have passed through a maze of tunnels," Zhong said. "My people know these tunnels well and use them if they are captured. They lead their captors into the maze. Once inside, my people run deeper into the maze. Their captors follow them and become completely lost and then die in these tunnels. The supplies are for my people after they escape."

Zhong's actions suddenly made sense. "So, you really did want them to follow us. You trapped them in the maze."

Before Zhong could answer, a violent shake of the ground threw us flat. Gravel showered down on our heads.

Zhong pulled the torch from the floor. "We must leave these tunnels now!"

We grabbed the bags and extra torches and ran across the cavern. We entered a tunnel opening just as another shake brought down the roof. Gravel and rocks sealed the tunnel behind us.

We followed our usual pattern through the tunnels, with Zhong leading, Mick behind him and me at the rear. We had been hiking through tunnels for what felt like days when Zhong said, "We are almost to the end of the tunnels."

"Good," Mick said. "Because I can't take much more of this.

The words had just left Mick's mouth when the tunnel shook with a power beyond anything I had felt before. Rocks and gravel came down in a torrent and buried us.

I dug upwards, seeking air and a way out. I found a narrow space under the tunnel roof. I took deep breaths of the dust-filled air and crawled into the space. I squeezed my way forward, hoping to reach the end of the tunnel Zhong had talked about. Another massive shake hit and didn't stop. My space filled with more rock and gravel. It trapped my arms. The only body part I could move was my head. I turned left and right, trying to find a pocket of air, but there was none.

A hand felt around my wrist, then grabbed it and pulled hard. I pushed with my feet and pulled with my free hand as best I could. I felt myself sliding forward, and then my head entered an open space. I gasped in thick air between hard coughs. The pull on my wrist continued, and my body eased into the space. When I was out, the hand released its grip. I remained motionless except for the coughing and waited for the quake to stop.

The violent shaking finally subsided until all that remained was a tremor. I brushed the gravel off my face and rolled up on an elbow. Zhong was beside me on a gravel slope, panting, his arm stretched out. Mick was motionless on the other side of Zhong. I was relieved when he coughed, confirming that he, too, had survived.

I looked around me. The air was thick with volcanic ash. We were in a large space filled with square huts. Every hut had collapsed and broken walls. None of the huts had roofs, and they appeared to have been built that way. I knew of only one village where the huts did not have roofs.

"We made it!" I shouted, my hoarse voice echoing. "We're in the Sanctuary!"

Zhong and Mick sat up slowly.

Mick coughed. "Where are the villagers?"

Zhong stood. "Come!"

We walked and slid down the gravel. As soon as we entered the village, the location of the villagers became obvious. Their motionless bodies were inside and between the huts and hidden under a thick layer of ash. We brushed away the ash and checked the bodies for pulses and breathing, but there was none. All the villagers were dead, with no signs of how they had died.

"What happened to them?" I asked.

"Toxic volcanic gases," Zhong said. He entered a hut and came out holding a mason's sledgehammer and chisel. "They are beyond our help. We must reach the Pathrakotau."

We ran across the open area between the village and the temples. On our left was a massive column of black smoke. It churned upwards from a huge hole that had been a hot volcanic lake before the eruption. The smoke column fed into the dark cloud we had seen surrounding the peak.

Ahead of us were large piles of black stones and broken roofs. They had been temples before their destruction. Our destination was the largest pile in the center. They were the remains of the largest temple, and the Pathrakotau—the Soul of the Beast, as we knew it—was in a large cavern behind it.

We picked our way up debris-covered steps to the temple and followed Zhong across the twisted roof to the back, where a small column of smoke streamed upwards. The smoke came from a hole blocked by a large back stone.

Zhong put the hammer and chisel down and grasped the stone. "We must move this out of the way"

To hold the stone, we all had to face into the smoke. Mick and I gagged from the stench of sulfur mixed with burnt flesh. We rolled the stone up and to the side. It created a space large enough for us to squeeze through. Zhong pushed his way inside head first. I passed him the chisel and the hammer. Then Mick and I squeezed in after him. Crawling on our bellies, Zhong led us around rocks and broken rafters toward an orange-red glow.

When we reached the glow, we could stand erect. We were at the top of stairs leading down to the cavern. We only saw the top steps, because a thick orange-red haze hid most of the stairs and the cavern.

With Zhong leading, we quickly descended the stairs and entered the haze. I could barely see Mick and the next step below me. I stepped onto the cavern floor where the visibility was slightly better. The floor was covered with ash and laced with orange-red cracks filled with hot lava, the source of the smoke and the light.

Zhong took us to the right at a fast pace and then stopped. The stench of burning flesh was stronger. He bent down and brushed ash and gravel away from something on the floor. It was a body with red clothing. Zhong brushed off two more bodies, also wearing red. The smell of burning flesh was from the bodies lying across the lava in the cracks.

"Monks," I said. "Whatever killed the villagers killed them, too."

"I do not think so," Zhong said and then froze. He was staring at a pulsing blue-white light that appeared to be floating in the haze.

"Zhong, you okay?" Mick whispered

Zhong didn't respond

"It's the Pathrakotau," I said. "It's taken hold of him."

"Are you sure?" Mick asked.

"I've seen that light before, It's coming from the diamond."

"You can't leave us now, Zhong," Mick said. He grabbed his shoulders and shook him.

Zhong looked around. "Thank you, Mick. I was not prepared."

"Prepared for what?" I asked.

"The power of the Pathrakotau. It is strong. It is what killed the monks."

I am prince of the world. The world belongs to me!

I looked around. "What was that?"

"What was what?" Mick asked.

Bow down. Worship me or die!

"There it is again! A voice. You must have heard it that time."

"What did it say?" Zhong asked.

"I'm a prince. The world is mine. Worship me or die."

"Whatever happens to me, you cannot stop," Zhong said. "You must complete our task."

"Don't even think about leaving us!" Mick said. "We need you, Zhong!"

"The hardest part of the task is over," Zhong replied. "We are here. The rest of the task is simple. Place the chisel at the base of each Begotten. Strike the chisel as hard as you can."

"Simple?" Mick said. "When has anything been simple?"

"You can do it," Zhong insisted. "Destiny would not have brought us this far to fail."

Zhong started across the bodies, Mick and I following reluctantly. The monks' bodies were crowded together like a thick, bumpy carpet. We stepped over them, except when there was no room for our feet.

The bodies continued up to the edge of the crevasse separating the Pathrakotau and its dragon statue from the rest of the cavern. The crevasse was filled to the brim with smoking red lava that overflowed its edges. The pulsing light was the only thing visible on the other side of the crevasse.

The light suddenly grew brighter, and the pulse rate sped up.

YOU DESCRATE MY TEMPLE! YOU SHALL ALL DIE!

"It's the voice!" I shouted.

The words were barely out of my mouth when a blinding blue-white flash knocked me flat. Everything went black.

I became aware of a pounding ache in my head. I opened my eyes to an orange-tinted fog. I was confused until the memory of where I was and what had happened flooded back. I raised myself on one elbow and stopped. I was too lightheaded to go higher. I couldn't see anything through the haze.

"Zhong? Mick?" I called with a raspy voice.

"Zhong's not moving!" Mick said from inside the haze to my right. "I think he's dead!"

I crawled toward Mick's voice. He was leaning over Zhong and feeling his neck and wrists for a pulse. I put my hands on Zhong's chest, hoping to feel shallow breathing. There was no movement. I tried to find a pulse. Still nothing.

"Anything?" Mick asked.

I shook my head. "He knew this would happen. This is what killed the monks."

"You know we can't do this without him," Mick said.

"We have to try."

I pried the chisel and hammer from Zhong's hands and handed the hammer to Mick. We staggered to our feet. I was still lightheaded and wobbly, but I remained standing. The blue-white light had returned to its normal brightness but continued to pulse rapidly.

Following the crevasse, we stepped over and on bodies until we reached the bridge to the other side. The bodies ended just before the bridge. The far half of the bridge was lost in the haze.

As we crossed the bridge, the huge dragon statue emerged from the smoke like a gray ghost. The ash had turned the dragon's upper body and wings a solid gray. The dragon's normal red and black were still visible on the undersurfaces. The statue's tail lay in pieces on the floor, but the rest of the statue appeared intact. Its two arms swept forward from under the dragon's wings. The claws came together under the dragon's open jaws to form a basket. Inside the basket was the reason we had come and why so many had died and would die if we failed.

Within the claw basket was a huge blue-white diamond shaped like a crouching bull. At its center was the pulsing light. It was the Pathrakotau, the sleeping god of the dragon men or, as the world knew it, the Soul of the Beast. The diamond was clear of the ash that covered everything else. The sides of the diamond moved in and out like heavy breathing. A web of cracks covering the diamond's surface spread and closed with each breath. Against all odds, I was sure we had arrived before the dragon god had completed its awakening.

"So, where do we cut?" Mick asked.

I stared at the diamond. "At the bases of the Begotten."

"And where is that?"

I shook my head in bewilderment. "I don't know."

We walked around the Pathrakotau and found small pits on both sides of the head, where a bull would have its horns. The egg-shaped diamond was in one of them. The tiger diamond was in the other. I grabbed the egg, and Mick gripped the tiger. We pulled and wiggled as hard as we could, but they wouldn't budge. They were fused with the Pathrakotau.

A large blue snake eye with a vertical yellow slit rolled up from the bottom of the diamond. Mick and I jumped back. The eye glared at us with pure hatred.

YOU DARE TO TOUCH ME! YOU SHALL DIE FOR THIS SACRILEGE!

"I heard it that time!" Mick said, readying the hammer. "Now or never, John!"

I placed the chisel at the base of the tiger.

"Ready, John?"

I nodded, not sure if I was.

Mick swung as hard as he could. The hammer hit the chisel with an echoing clang. A bone-jarring shock shot up my arm. Blue-white light burst from the Pathrakotau. A deep stabbing pain went through my head, and then everything went black—again.

The ground beneath me shook and rolled. I opened my eyes and then shut them against a blinding blue-white light. I put a hand over my eyes and looked between my fingers. The Pathrakotau had become a perfect sphere, five times its normal size. Squinting against the light, I felt around me and found the chisel and then Mick's body. I shook his shoulder

"Mick, wake up!"

""Ohh…"Mick groaned.

"Mick, you still have the hammer?"

"Yeah, I got it."

"I've got the chisel," I said. "We've got to try again, now! The Pathrakotau's about to explode!"

We used the claws of the basket to pull ourselves up, blinking to see into the intense light

I HAVE AWAKENED! THE WORLD IS MINE!

"We're too late" Mick shouted. "It's awake!"

"It's lying! We try again!"

"And where do we hit it, John? The last place didn't work. And now we can't see anything!"

Whatever we were going to do, we had to do it now. I knew the only way to cut a diamond was to strike it in exactly the right spot. That's why our last hit had failed. But finding the exact spot on a diamond was impossible, especially if we couldn't see.

A huge hand surrounded my hand with the chisel and placed it on the Pathrakotau. I didn't know what this was, but it was our only hope. "Strike the chisel, Mick!" I shouted. "I've got the chisel in place!"

"John, I can't see!"

"I don't care! Just do it! Swing!"

CLANG! CRACK! I felt a jolt in my arm like it had been ripped off.

The huge hand repositioned my hand and the chisel. Mick's hammer pounded the chisel, sending another jolt up my arm.

An explosion of blue-white light sent me flying. My head slammed against the hard ground.

A scream echoed wildly around me. "AHHHHHHHahhhhhhhhhAHHHHHHH!"

Oblivion was sucking me down when a burning pain in my face pulled me back. I forced my eyes open. Inches from my face, and oozing closer, was red-hot lava from the crevasse. I was about to be burned alive. I tried to move away, but my body would not obey my brain, and my eyes closed against my will.

Something slipped under my chest and legs and lifted me into the air. The heat on my face disappeared, and I felt a gentle swaying. I had to know what was happening. I fought to open my eyes one last time. Above me was the head of a huge beardless man with long blond hair. His calm face stared straight ahead and gave me a sense of total peace and safety.

I had never been close enough to see the face of Simon's protector; none of us had. Looking up from below, I still didn't see his face clearly, but I knew it was him. Like the time I saw the prophet's statue, I knew I had seen his face before.

Just as I lost the strength to resist the waiting blackness, the protector looked down at me and smiled. His eyes shocked me, and the pieces of the puzzle suddenly snapped together. My last thought before slipping into blackness was, *that's impossible.*

CHAPTER FOURTEEN

"John, wake up."

The voice shocked me. I tried to sit up, but a wave of nausea and dizziness made me lie back down. "I thought you were dead," I said.

"I was very close," Zhong replied. He held a flickering torch that outlined his calm face.

Another face came into view. "Mick," I said. "We made it. All of us."

I noticed their faces were easy to see. That's when I realized the haze in the cavern was gone, and the tremors had stopped.

"How long was I out?"

"We were all unconscious for days," Zhong said. He held a water bag to my lips, and I drank. "You've been unconscious the longest."

"What about the Pathrakotau?"

"If you're asking did you and Mick stop the awakening, you did. You struck the Begotten in the precise locations to split them off. I do not know how you found them."

"I didn't find them—someone moved my hand."

"That same someone helped me, too," Mick said. "I couldn't see anything. Then a big hand grabbed my hand, and, next thing I know, I'm swinging the hammer."

I pushed myself up. Zhong and Mick took an arm and helped me to sit. I was still a little light-headed but getting better.

The crevasse was fifteen feet away and empty. The lava in the crevasse and the floor cracks was gone. The cavern was illuminated by Zhong's torch and six moving torches on the other side of the crevasse. I felt a sharp pain on my face. It stung when I touched it.

"Your face is burned," Zhong said

That stirred up the memory. "There was an explosion. It threw me right next to the crevasse. I remember the lava was almost touching my face, but I couldn't move."

"Then how did you get here?" Mick asked.

"He lifted me and carried me away from the lava."

"Who lifted you?" Zhong asked

"Simon's protector," I said. "I'm sure it was him."

"If he was here, then he's the one who guided your hand and Mick's when you cut out the Begotten."

"Zhong, I saw his face," I said. "You'll never guess who he is."

"Simon," Zhong said quietly.

"That's right. How did you know?"

"The Protector and Simon have been strongly connected since Simon's birth."

"Do you realize what that means?" Mick asked. "When the Protector saved baby Simon from being sacrificed, Simon was actually saving himself."

"This just gets stranger and stranger," I said.

"We all knew Simon was unique," Zhong said. "What we didn't know was the depth of it."

I pointed to the moving torches "Where did they come from?"

Zhong glanced at them. "They are the surviving villagers. When the volcano erupted, they were in the valley with the mists we rode through. That is where we grow most of our food. One half of the villagers are always at work in the valley. We are fortunate the main tunnel between the Sanctuary and the valley is still open."

"I thought your food came from gardens in the village," Mick said.

"The gardens are too small to supply all our needs."

"What are the villagers doing?" I asked.

"They carry our dead to the village for cremation. I was awakened when they laid me on a funeral pyre."

Mick chuckled. "That must've been a shock."

Zhong nodded. "For them and me."

"Did any monks survive?" I asked

"No. I am the only living monk in the Sanctuary."

"Don't take this the wrong way," Mick said, "but how did you survive and they didn't?"

"I saw that the monks were not physically injured. They were all facing toward the Pathrakotau. When I felt its power, I knew the monks died from a mental attack they did not expect and were not prepared for. I prepared immediately. When the Pathrakotau attacked again, I went deep inside."

"Then why are John and I still alive?" Mick asked. "We weren't prepared. We don't even know what prepared means."

"I suspect you both have a natural resistance to mental control and attack," Zhong said. "That is why destiny chose you for this task. But the most important difference between the monks and you is our meditations. I believe the meditations opened us to the attack."

I tried to stand. "I need to see the Pathrakotau."

With Zhong's help, Mick and I stood. Then I held onto the claw basket to steady myself. Zhong held the torch over the basket while we looked inside.

The undersurfaces of the dragon statue's head and neck and the inside of the claw basket were scorched black. The huge diamond had split down the middle from nose to tail, and the two halves had fallen apart. The clear blue-white of the diamond had turned an opaque gray. The pulsing light inside was gone.

"I don't know what a dead god looks like," Mick said, "but that sure looks like one to me."

"What would happen if we pushed the halves together?" I asked.

"An important question," Zhong said. "Would they fuse? Would that allow the dragon god to begin another awakening? No one knows."

"Well, if there's any chance of it coming back," Mick said, "I say crush the Pathrakotau, and scatter the pieces."

"That is a matter for the next priests to decide," Zhong said. "We should go to the village. They have a place where we can recover. Mick and I will help you, John."

We staggered across the cavern floor and then climbed the stairs leading out of the cavern. Halfway up, we stepped aside to make room for two villagers carrying out a monk's body. At the top of the stairs was a wide path under the collapsed roof. The rocks and timbers had been cleared to make enough room for the villagers to carry out the dead. Once outside, we followed the cleared path down the steps and across the open area to the village.

The air was now clear. While crossing the open area, I took my first good look at the Sanctuary. There wasn't a hut in the village that didn't have at least one collapsed wall. Where the column of volcanic smoke had been was a massive crater. It was empty, except for a few narrow plumes of smoke.

The rock beach that once bordered a volcanic lake had twelve funeral pyres. Four of the pyres were actively burning and cremating the dead piled on the top. Four pyres were blackened, smoking heaps surrounded by villagers collecting the ashes of the deceased. The last four pyres were being rebuilt with fresh wood.

Any villagers not working were sleeping or eating in an area next to the village. We collapsed beside the resting villagers. After we drank and ate, we also slept.

When we awoke the next morning, we were strong enough to help the villagers. We built the funeral pyres. We carried bodies. We piled the dead on the new pyres. The only task we didn't do was collect the ashes. It was a sacred act that only a villager could perform. It had been a tradition of the Sanctuary for centuries.

It took another week to collect and cremate all the bodies. We stood with the remaining villagers in front of the last unburned funeral pyre. Zhong, Mick and I were the only ones with torches, because we were to light the wood. The villagers were honoring us for stopping the awakening of the dragon god.

At a nod from the village elder, we pushed our torches into the pyre. Then we stepped back. The fire spread and quickly and became a tall column of flame and smoke. The smoke ascended to the top of the volcanic cone. Everyone stood silently and watched the flames until all that remained was a smoking pile of ashes.

The villagers formed into a long column behind Zhong, Mick and me. With a nod from Zhong, we led them to the rest area. Everyone sat in their usual locations without speaking. The villagers' silence was partly from the exhaustion of completing a long strenuous task but mostly from the emotional pain of losing family and friends. Until that moment, the villagers had been too busy to grieve.

"Strange," Mick said quietly.

I looked at him. "What is?"

"How so much has happened, and then it all just ends with barely a whimper."

"That is life," Zhong said. "Most of the world's greatest events pass into obscurity, their importance completely forgotten."

"Will they rebuild the Sanctuary?" I asked.

"The villagers begin tomorrow. They will start with the village and then construct the main temple. Five of the villagers will begin their preparations to become priests. A summons will be sent to a monk in the world to return and become their teacher."

"Why don't you do it, Zhong?" Mick asked. "You're a great teacher, and you're already here."

"I have blood on my hands," Zhong said. "The monk who returns has never killed."

"I'm sorry, Zhong," I said.

"For what?"

"For all the killing you did to do to protect Mick and me."

"I have no regrets," Zhong replied. "And neither should you. I was faithful to my destiny."

"Any idea what they'll do with the Pathrakotau?" Mick asked.

"I know that many villagers agree with you," Zhong said. "But as I told you, that is a decision the monks must make. Regardless of what they decide, the Pathrakotau's destiny cannot be changed."

Over the last several days, I'd had a growing sense of something that needed to be done. Suddenly, I knew what it was. "We have to find out what happened."

"What do you mean?" Mick asked.

"The war! We need to know who won. What happened to our army and the prophet and his army."

"I agree," Mick said. "What do you say, Zhong?"

"Our work here is finished," Zhong replied. "We may leave whenever we choose."

"Then let's leave now," I said.

"Now?" Mick asked. "As in, just get up and leave?"

"Yes. Now."

Zhong stood. "I will tell the village elder."

CHAPTER FIFTEEN

Zhong, Mick and I halted our Arabian horses at the top of a sand dune. A mile to the west was the Gulf of Suez. We were at the location of our army's first defensive line. The sand ahead of us was as empty as the hundreds of miles behind us. Like everywhere we had been, we saw no sign that a battle had ever happened.

Mick shook his head in disbelief. "How do you hide a war?"

"You can't," I said.

"So, it was all just hallucinations?"

"Some people would say that."

After leaving the Himalayas, we had traveled by train to Bombay and then by sea to the Arabian Peninsula. We bought the horses and supplies we needed and rode west across the Arabian and Sinai peninsulas, following the expected path of our army's fighting retreat.

We had questioned almost every person we encountered, hoping to learn the outcome of the war. Everyone denied any knowledge of a recent battle. At first, we thought they were lying. But when we spoke with more people and kept hearing the same thing, we realized they were telling the truth.

After that, our purpose changed to finding proof that the war had happened and that we weren't insane. Armies and battles always leave plentiful evidence: bullet casings, knives, guns, canteens, clothing, coins, discarded equipment, trash, letters and faded pictures. We had stopped at hundreds of likely locations to walk and dig the ground. We had found nothing.

"I should do this alone," Zhong said.

He rode down the front of the dune and then across the sand toward the gulf. He leaned to his right and left to study the ground. When he was several hundred yards away, he dismounted and began digging into the sand. He found something and put it in his pocket. He remounted his horse and trotted back to us.

He halted beside us and lifted a sandy lump out of his pocket. He brushed off the sand, exposing something black.

"Tar from the Greek fire," Zhong said.

"Then we're not crazy," Mick said.

Zhong shook his head. "No, we are not."

"Then why don't people remember?" I asked.

"I do not know."

Mick looked around. "Do we keep going?"

"No," Zhong replied. "Our search ends here."

"Then I suggest we travel to England," I said. "I have a fortune, and each of you shall have a third."

"John, we're going with you," Mick said, "but I don't need or want that kind of money. Just give me enough for my needs, and I'll be fine."

"You know I must refuse all money," Zhong said. "A rich servant is not invisible."

"I can't force it on you," I said. "But the money's still yours. It'll be in accounts with your names."

"Let's sort it out when we get there," Mick said. "I say it's time to find a ship and hope the next voyage goes better than the last one."

"Zhong, we're close to the pyramids at Giza," I said. "You still haven't seen them."

"If it is your wish to visit the pyramids, then we should go there," Zhong replied. "But please, do not visit the pyramids on my account. I have developed a strong dislike of pyramids."

"Zhong, did you just tell a joke?" Mick asked.

Zhong smiled.

Mick and I burst out laughing.

General Tong Rhongi
National Army Headquarters
Nanching, Kiangsu Province
August 23, 1933

Dear Sir John,

You are no more surprised to receive this letter than I am to write it. After the Dragon War, I inquired after you and your friends many times but never found anyone who knew of you.

I do not remember how it happened, but your name came up during a recent consultation with a friend of yours, Sir Harold Cummings of the British consulate. Needless to say, I was delighted to learn you are alive and well. He agreed to forward my letter to you through the consular mail. I inquired regarding Zhong and Mick, but Sir Harold did not know their names. He did mention that you had an Oriental servant. I knew the servant was Zhong. Remembering your need for secrecy, I did not inquire further.

As for me, after the Dragon War, I returned to China and rejoined the national army. I am a minister of my government, and we are in a fight for our lives against the Japanese. Unfortunately, the war does not go well, and we are in a forced retreat to the south.

I assume you have returned to the sites where we fought and found that all memories and evidence of the war have disappeared. It began just weeks after the final battle. Anytime I mentioned the Dragon

War, I was met with blank stares and statements to the effect that I was mistaken. When I insisted the war had happened, they would ask how a recent war of that magnitude could be known to no one but myself. An excellent question, and one for which I did not have an answer.

Hoping to find a reason for this amnesia, I returned to the Sinai and Arabian peninsulas and walked the ground over which we fought. I looked everywhere for proof of the war, but even the desert had forgotten. I found nothing except sand. All physical proof of the war had vanished.

I can understand how the physical evidence could be eliminated, but how do you remove the memories of thousands? It is impossible, except for the fact that it happened. Finally, convinced that further discussion was futile, I have not talked or written about the Dragon War for decades.

Since you cannot know what happened after you left for India. I will describe the main events.

Minutes after you rode off, a giant gray dragon arose at the center of the enemy's army. The beast inspired the dragon men to attack like Sun Tzu's thunderbolt. They were about to overrun us when Simon, once again, became the Golden Warrior. He charged the dragon, and they collided with an explosion greater than anything I have ever experienced.

Our army was stunned, but we all survived. The Golden Warrior, the dragon and every dragon soldier within a 1,000-yard radius of the explosion vanished. The remainder of the dragon army was as stunned, as we were. The remaining dragon men panicked and ran. We pursued them and killed them until we collapsed. That was a glorious victory, and we have Simon to thank for it.

We had just finished repairing our defensive line when the dragon army attacked again, this time without their precious dragon. We killed them by the tens of thousands, but they kept coming. Eventually, their numbers overwhelmed us. We were forced to withdraw and begin a fighting retreat across the Sinai and Arabian peninsulas. Our soldiers willingly spent their blood and lives to buy you the time to reach the Soul of the Beast.

We were on the verge of annihilation when the dragon men halted their advance and built a defensive line six hundred yards west of our position. Our scouts reported that, behind their line, thousands of dragon men were digging like madmen into the sand. After three days, they unearthed the remains of the third temple. It was exactly where Zhong's analysis said it would be.

That is when the prophet arrived. He entered the temple, and that was our most terrible moment. We were certain all our efforts and sacrifices had been for nothing, that you had failed to reach the Soul of the Beast, that the dragon god would soon awaken.

Then the dragon men suddenly abandoned their defenses and ran to the west. There was only one explanation. You had just destroyed the Soul of the Beast and stopped the awakening. I did not have to rally our army. They shouted and charged with new energy. So began another wave of killing.

As we swept past the temple, I led a company of soldiers inside. We found a circle of dragon men around the prophet as he kneeled before a statue of a dragon. My men and I killed the dragon men. Then I ran my sword through the prophet's heart. I enjoyed watching him bleed and die before his god, like so many of his victims.

I sent men to retrieve as much gunpowder as possible. I would have preferred Simon's powder, but there was none to be had. We placed the gunpowder inside the temple, and I lit a long fuse. Then we rejoined the attack. Twenty minutes later, there was a massive explosion to our rear. A huge gray cloud rose into the sky. The third temple will never be used again.

I am certain you wish to know about Shareef. He died during our retreat. I buried him deep in the sand with my own hands. I left his grave unmarked. As for Simon, there is nothing more to tell. I honor his memory. Simon was a truly great warrior, as are the three of you.

Even though I have not spoken about the war for decades, I think about it often. I have concluded that the powers that eliminated the proof and memory of the dragon war are the same powers that attempted to awaken the dragon god.

I believe those powers are maneuvering the world's events for a second attempt at the awakening. If I am correct, your knowledge of the enemy must be available to those who fight the next awakening. As Sun Tzu wisely taught, a people who do not know their enemy will be defeated.

I have written my memoirs of the war and have hidden them for the time when they are needed. The parts that you, Zhong and Mick played are far more crucial than mine. I urge you to record the events you experienced. They, too, must be there when the world needs to remember.

I have heard rumors of a coming war with Germany. May Destiny protect us now as it did then.

Forever your comrade-in-arms,
Tong Rhongi
General, Minister of War

EPILOGUE

I ended this journal sooner and more abruptly than I intended. I apologize, but I had no choice. The workers in my study have almost finished the false wall. They are now waiting for me to place my strong box inside. Once I do, they will plaster and paint the remaining hole. The workers believe I am an eccentric old man hiding his will, because that is what I led them to believe.

Since you are reading this, you know about the false wall and this journal. You probably wonder why I broke my vow to never speak or write about the Sanctuary. I kept my vow until several years ago. That was when a letter arrived from an unexpected source: Tong Rhongi.

His letter described the events of the war after we left for the Sanctuary. Tong Rhongi wrote of his concern that if the dragon god makes another attempt to awaken, the world will need our hard-earned knowledge to stop it. Without that knowledge, the dragon god may succeed. Tong Rhongi's feelings reinforced a growing unease I have had about a future reawakening. That is why I wrote this journal.

To keep my vow, I only wrote when I was alone, and I always kept my writings in my safe. Once I place this journal inside the false wall, I leave it to Destiny to reveal the hiding place and my journal at the time when it is needed.

I never discussed the journal with Zhong, but he knows it exists. I could never hide anything from him. Knowing Zhong as I do, I am certain he agrees with my decision. By not bringing the journal to his official attention, Zhong is not obligated to stop me. Thus, he does not break his vow.

Once this journal is revealed, the time of the dragon god's reawakening is near. If you think you found this journal by chance and the coming awakening is something you can ignore, you are wrong. Destiny has chosen you for the tasks ahead. Should you try to ignore or escape your destiny, you will not succeed. Zhong, Mick and I are witnesses to that.

I have included Tong Rhongi's letter in this strong box. It discusses events of the war of which I was previously unaware. They may be of importance to you. I pray that Zhong and I have both acted correctly and honorably.

Sincerely,
John L. Sexton, Esq.
April 21, 1936